SWIMMING TO
CHICAGO

Praise for David-Matthew Barnes

Swimming to Chicago

"[A]n interesting contemporary novel...I found myself unable to put it down..."—Sara Power, *Books Your Kids Will Love*

Mesmerized

"Barnes's young adult novel about two boys suddenly, deeply in love has a fairy-tale tone, but it will strike all the right notes for YA readers as the boys dance into the hearts of The Showdown audience."—Richard Labonte, *BookMarks*

"There is a wonderful resounding theme: sometimes you have to be brave enough to love and forgive. You won't grasp these words completely unless you read this entire heartrending story..."—*QMO (Queer Magazine Online)*

"[R]elevant to the plight of many gay teens...a vivid and realistic telling of the emotions and unfortunate realities that can face a teenager in reconciling his sexuality...very well written...four stars..."—Bob Lind, *Echo Magazine*

"[A] timely work that will resonate with readers for its portrayal of society's perception of the GLBT community."—*Out & About*

"[A] teenage love story, but it's between Brodie and Lance... it explores grief and loss—particularly the difference between having a loved one murdered and choosing to reject someone for being gay."—Kel Munger, *Sacramento News & Review*

By the Author

Mesmerized

Accidents Never Happen

Swimming to Chicago

SWIMMING TO CHICAGO

by

David-Matthew Barnes

A Division of Bold Strokes Books

2011

SWIMMING TO CHICAGO
© 2011 By David-Matthew Barnes. All Rights Reserved.

ISBN 13: 978-1-60282-572-7

This Trade Paperback Original Is Published By
Bold Strokes Books, Inc.
P.O. Box 249
Valley Falls, NY 12185

First Edition: October 2011

CREDITS
EDITORS: GREG HERREN AND STACIA SEAMAN
PRODUCTION DESIGN: STACIA SEAMAN
COVER DESIGN BY SHERI (GRAPHICARTIST2020@HOTMAIL.COM)

Acknowledgments

Many people helped bring *Swimming to Chicago* to print. To them, I offer my deepest gratitude:

To Len Barot, for her unconditional support, shared wisdom, and never-ending faith in my stories.

To Greg Herren, for being a genius editor, a patient teacher, and a brilliant writer.

To the wonderful Bold Strokes Books family, especially Cindy Cresap, Connie Ward, Kim Baldwin, Lori Anderson, Ruth Sternglantz, Sandy Lowe, Sheri, and Stacia Seaman.

To Emily Haines and the members of Metric, for providing the perfect soundtrack to this novel, without even realizing it.

To Shirley Manson for her beauty, strength, and truth.

For their never-ending support and words of encouragement: Aaron Martinez, Albert Magana, Billie Parish, Carsen Taite, Collin Kelley, Danielle Downs, Debra Garnes, Elizabeth Warren, Frankie Hernandez, Jamie Hughes, Jill McMahon, Jodi Blue, Karen Head, Kate Williams, Kelly Wilson Lopez, Kimberly Faye Greenberg, Leila Wells Rogers, Linda Velasco Wread, Liz Hawkins Jester, Lynn Furtal, Marilyn Montague, Michelle Boman Harris, Nance Haxton, Nita Manley, Patricia Abbott-Dinsmore, Rebecca Johnson, Robyn Colburn, Sabra Rahel, Selena Ambush, Stefani Deoul, Susan Madden, Tara Henry, Therease Logan, and Todd Wylie.

To my parents, Samuel Barnes, Jr. and Nancy Nickle, and my brothers, Jamin, Jason, Andy, and Jaren, for allowing me to be the writer in the family.

To my students, who teach me more on a daily basis than I could ever dream of teaching them.

To the loving memory of my grandmother, Dorothy Helen Nickle, for my childhood of soap operas and tea parties.

To Nick A. Moreno, who believed in this story (and me) long before I did.

To Mindy Morgan, for being my best friend for over twenty years.

To Rena Mason, for always having my back.

To Stacy Scranton, for always knowing the right thing to say.

To Cyndi Lopez and Bethany Hidden-Cauley, for being sassy and sexy.

To Edward C. Ortiz, for the wonderful life and love we share.

To the beautiful city of Chicago. And the always inspiring people who live there.

To God, for everything. Without You, I'm nothing.

In loving memory of

Norman Michael Parent
June 28, 1988–September 18, 2009

Because you lived and loved without fear.

I am not young enough to know everything.
—Oscar Wilde

Part One

June/Hunis

JILLIAN

Summer started like a seduction. They saw glimpses of it in late May, peeking through windows and dancing across every lawn in Harmonville. It snuck into their lives, flirting and tempting them with freedom from school, boredom, and homework. It was thick with promises of excitement, and hot possibilities of romance and sex.

Like parolees, Jillian Dambro and Alex Bainbridge lapped up the start of summer vacation with a frenzied desire to explore all they'd missed while confined by nine months of high school. Every second of every day was filled with as much activity as possible. They were making up for lost time as though terrified of dying at the age of seventeen. But by the day the season officially began in the third week of June, their lust for life had faded. Apathy arrived like an uninvited houseguest. They slept late, watched too much television, and ate whatever they wanted—while doing their best to dodge questions about college applications.

Jillian noticed Alex was avoiding *everyone's* questions— even hers.

She knew something was wrong. After eleven years of friendship, she could just tell. She secretly cussed herself out for not having the courage to casually bring up her concerns in their daily conversations. *I'm a shitty friend*, she told herself. *I need to stop being so selfish.*

A hollow coldness had crept into Alex's eyes, and it scared Jillian. There was a sense of anger shadowing him, like an imaginary friend playing a cruel and constant game of piggyback. He carried bitterness around with him. His hands gripped everything they touched with frustration. The edges of his words ended with a bristling sharpness, carrying an unspoken caution that he shouldn't be challenged. It was in every step he took—his stride was mean and severe as he pounded the earth in his favorite pair of black and white Converse shoes. The rage seemed permanent, as if he were possessed by something trying to escape from his body. It seeped out of his soul through an insensitive stare.

Jillian became crippled with fear her friendship with Alex was falling apart, and she couldn't figure out why.

She was overwhelmed by this abrupt sense of loss one Friday afternoon. She sat on the sofa wearing a pink and white gingham tank top and white Capris, remote control in hand. The opening theme music to *The Young and the Restless* blared from the outdated television set. Her bare feet were resting on the lip of the marred coffee table. She wiggled her freshly painted toes, noticing the new sandals she'd bought last week were giving the tops of her feet a strange V-shaped tan line. She tightened her ponytail by grabbing two thick strands of her honey-colored hair and pulling firmly. She'd been toying with the idea of changing her image. She wanted to dye her hair jet black. And get colored contacts—green, probably—because she was tired of her brown eyes. All new makeup, and all new clothes.

She wanted to become a new person.

Jillian reached for an ice-cold bottle of Wild Cherry Pepsi on the lamp table to her right. She unscrewed the cap, took a sip, and welcomed the sweet burn of the soda in her throat. She was craving a cigarette but had to wait until her mother left for work so she could smoke in peace, without the risk of getting grounded again. "Hurry up," she said quietly, hoping the hushed words would somehow urge her mother to get out of the house.

"Baby!" Delilah Dambro called from the other room. Jillian cringed at the sound of the husky, throaty voice. Her mother had a knack for destroying the English language with her tacky euphemisms and out-of-control Southern accent. "You seen my purse, buttercup?"

"You left it in the car."

"What'd you say, sugar?"

"You left it in the car!" Jillian practically screamed.

She could hear her klutzy mother stumble down the hallway before stepping down into the sunken living room. "Darlin', I really wish you wouldn't yell like that."

Jillian didn't take her eyes from the television screen. "I didn't realize you were teaching etiquette lessons now."

Delilah sighed a little. "You, little girl, have the manners of a dairy cow. Get your filthy feet off of my coffee table."

The realization hit Jillian then. It swept over her like an allergic reaction. Her eyes narrowed, suddenly sensitive to the sunshine tumbling in from the front window and spilling all over the worn carpet of the living room. Her chest burned and her breath caught in her throat. Her pulse throbbed and pounded in her wrists and temples. She felt sweat forming on the back of her knees and a slow, growing wave of nausea in the pit of her stomach. *Alex is hiding something from me. Something serious.*

Jillian sensed her mother's look of concern. "You all right?" she asked.

"Yes…"

"You don't look well." Delilah folded her arms across her chest. She quickly unfolded them, saying "Dang gone it" when she smashed her waitress name tag against her left boob. She shot Jillian a wide-eyed look. "Good Lord, you're not pregnant, are you?"

Jillian rolled her eyes, and said through a smirk, "Must've been all the whiskey I drank last night."

Delilah didn't blink, trying to appear in control of the situation. "Good for you, sister. Drink yourself to death like your granny did. She was a party girl, too." Delilah returned to the task of finding her missing purse. She sauntered off. Seconds later, Jillian could hear her mother's black high heels scuffing across the kitchen floor. The door leading from the house to the garage creaked open. "That cheap stuff always kicks you in the ass, honey bee! Jesus Christ, this garage is a filthy mess. Look at all this crap. Useless junk left behind by a useless man."

Jillian sat up, placed both feet on the floor, and tossed the remote control aside. "My God...I'm losing my best friend." She stood up, scanning the room for the black cordless phone.

Delilah came back into the room, her right hand wrapped through the shoulder strap of her faux leather purse. She smoothed out a few wrinkles in her uniform. "What's the matter? You lose somethin'?"

Jillian stopped for a moment and took a deep look at her mother. Jillian thought her mother was way too thin. As usual, Delilah also had on too much blush, and her cheap perfume swam around the room. "I think so," Jillian breathed. "But you wouldn't understand."

Delilah ran a few fingers through her burgundy-tinted hair. Her long nails, painted a vibrant shade of peach, snagged on a couple of fresh curls. Jillian thought her mother looked like a sad clown, an escapee from some cruel circus. "I look all right?"

Jillian purposely avoided her mother's eyes. "Have you seen the cordless? My cell phone died and I forgot to charge it."

"It's in the bathroom. I was talking to Conner while I was curling my hair."

Jillian couldn't help herself. "You've got too much blush on."

"I do?" Delilah opened her purse, searching for her compact. "I might be home late tonight, buttercup. Conner wants to take me out...for drinks. Ain't that sweet?" She studied her reflection in the round mirror. She rubbed a little at her cheeks. "There...that's better."

"Sure it is," Jillian said with a forced grin. She moved past her mother, went inside the bathroom at the end of the hall, and shut the door.

❖

Jillian sat on the edge of the bathtub, her feet and toes sinking into a bubble-gum pink shaggy floor mat. She looked over to the cluttered sink and noticed her mother had forgotten to turn off her curling iron. She picked up the black cordless phone, dialed a memorized number, and waited for an answer.

"Hello?" he said, gruff.

"You were sleeping."

"I know. My mom's on my ass about it, too. She says we gotta find something *productive* for me to do this summer." Jillian could hear the frosty edge to his words and the frustration in his breath. She was determined to have a normal conversation with him. She needed to, so her fear they were drifting apart could be dismissed.

"Tell your mother she needs to mind her own business."

"You know she's been depressed, Jilli. I'll just try to avoid her until August. I want to avoid everyone."

Jillian wondered if he meant her as well. She swallowed and said, "The summer is going by too fast. Only nine and a half more weeks."

He sighed, bored. "I just wanna get the next year over with."

Jillian stood up, went to the mirror above the sink. She opened her mouth, running an index finger across her teeth. She felt nervous, fidgety. "My car's still in the shop. They're holding it hostage until I pay them a ridiculous amount of money. I'm tired of walking everywhere and bumming rides from people. I need to find a job."

"Yeah, well, I wish I could quit mine." Just a week ago, Alex had gushed over his new job, thrilled about an unexpected raise. Jillian was more certain than ever that something was wrong. She knew they needed to spend more time together, to prevent the distance from growing.

"Hey," she said with feigned enthusiasm, "ask Mr. Freeman if he'll hire me. Tell him I'll even consider going out with his bonehead son if he does. It can't be that difficult to make a pizza."

Alex coughed, cleared his throat. "Sue Ellen already beat you to it. She's waiting tables."

"Ah, nepotism has found its way into the lovely state of Georgia." Jillian opened the medicine cabinet, reading the labels on her mother's bottles of prescribed drugs. Too many tranquilizers. "I hate Sue Ellen Freeman. That bitch told me I looked like a boy."

"That was almost three years ago."

"So?"

"So, you've got tits now."

Jillian glanced down at her chest. "Yeah," she said, with a small laugh. "Barely."

Alex cut right to the point. "Why are you calling me?"

She winced a little, shut the medicine cabinet, and turned off her mother's curling iron. "Can't I call my best friend on a Friday afternoon?"

"If you want me to come over, just say so."

She held her breath for a moment before asking, "Will you?"

Alex was silent for a second on the other end. The pause scared Jillian. They'd always talked about everything. There had never been secrets between them. Ever. "I got some stuff I have to do around the house first. I think my mom's lonely. I need to help her with a few things. Keep her company for a while."

"My mom went to work," she offered.

"The Queen of Applebee's?"

"She loves that place. She gets to make waitresses younger than her feel like shit five days a week."

"Maybe you should get a job there." His words cut deep. Alex knew how much Jillian disliked her mother's working-class ways, and the fact she'd settled for a boring, routine life in a boring, routine town.

She tried to control the venom in her voice. "I'm not exactly waitress material. I'm saving myself for life in a big city."

Alex moved in for the kill. "You can always work at Value Mart."

Jillian wasn't sure what she'd done to deserve that. "I'd rather die than work there."

ALEX

After hanging up the phone, Alex stayed in bed and stared up at his bedroom ceiling. He welcomed the cool comfort of the blue cotton sheets against his legs and arms. The electric hum of the air conditioner spouting a cold breeze through a duct above his bedroom door offered him a strange sense of security.

His mother's contagious laughter floated upstairs from the kitchen below. She was on the phone, talking to one of their relatives in Chicago. Alex strained to hear the Armenian words his mother spoke. He wasn't fluent, but knew enough to know she was defending the reputation of a promiscuous girl and giving her the benefit of the doubt. He loved to hear her speak in Armenian. Her voice always lifted, thick with happiness and truth. Lately, she seemed unusually sad and distant. The soft waves of her rock-smoothing laughter were a relief.

Alex replayed his phone conversation with Jillian in his mind. He knew she was concerned about him. He could hear it in her voice as she had tried her best to make him laugh, to find the source of his anxiety. Her gentle reminders she was still his best friend made him love her even more.

Alex's guilt roamed through his veins like ghosts looting an old house. It wasn't Jillian's fault. She had no idea what was going on. He knew he'd been unusually mean to her, so he vowed to make it up to her by being a better friend. Although she pretended to be tough, Alex knew firsthand how sensitive Jillian was, how much she relied on him. There was a connection between the two of them carrying a deeper meaning than Alex could understand or define.

He wondered what her reaction would be when he told her the truth—nothing in his life had been the same since last Saturday when Tommy Freeman spent the night.

For the last week, Alex had tried to hide out from everyone. He was constantly being reminded he was a different person now. He was frightened others might be able to see it—they could tell what he'd done just by looking at him. Everywhere he went, he felt haunted by shame. He walked with his shoulders slumped forward, his eyes to the ground, his hands in his pockets. He avoided stares, turning away from people as quickly as possible. He retreated to his bedroom, searching for solace by listening to his favorite band Metric on his headphones, playing games on his cell phone or rereading his favorite comic book for the four hundredth time. He caught distorted glimpses of himself in the mocking faces of clocks and watches, in the finger-smudged glass of bathroom mirrors, in reflections of the greasy forks and spoons in the kitchen at work. Alex felt the constant need to escape from the relentless images. He didn't recognize himself. He had no idea who he was anymore. In his mind, he'd simultaneously become a bounty hunter and a fugitive, victim, and villain. There was a new disdain burning inside him, a powerful dislike he carried like a pistol aimed at his tortured heart. The self-hatred caught in his throat when he spoke, leaving a residue of chalk and vinegar on the back of his tongue. It found a spot to hide between his teeth and gums like chewing tobacco, stuck snugly between his shoulder blades while he slept.

Alex turned over on his left side, facing the double accordion doors of his closet. He closed his eyes, remembering what it had felt like when Tommy Freeman was next to him in bed.

❖

The room had been dark and wrapped in the young sweetness of dawn. Alex was lying on the edge of the bed, listening to the melodic rhythm of Tommy's breathing and facing his closet, his bedroom door, and the massive poster of Metric's lead singer Emily Haines covering half of the wall.

While Tommy slept, Alex found a source to calm his nerves: reciting all of the lyrics to his favorite Metric songs in his mind, starting with "Help, I'm Alive" and ending with "Poster of a Girl."

Why am I so nervous? he thought in between the songs playing in his mental jukebox. *It's just Tommy Freeman. We've been friends forever. Hell, we work together.*

Alex tried desperately to ignore the nagging desire he felt to be close to Tommy. The boys were lying back to back. Tommy was facing the wall. The tips of Tommy's toes were near the edge of the windowsill. Alex felt wired, unusually alert. His eyes darted around the room, squinting and trying to make out Emily's frozen features in the sallow summer sunrise.

Alex felt guilty. He wanted to look at Tommy. He wanted to study his face. He wanted to touch the slightly curled edges of his dark blond hair. He wanted to scoot back a little so their spines were touching. He wanted to roll over and kiss the back of Tommy's neck. Alex just couldn't figure out why he was having these thoughts.

Alex's shoulders tightened as Tommy suddenly turned over and draped a casual, sleepy arm around his waist. He could feel the warmth of Tommy's palm and fingertips, resting against his stomach, just inches above the waistband of his boxers. Tommy's mouth, his full lips, hovered delicately over the nape of Alex's neck. Alex's heart began to pound so fast and loud he was certain it would wake Tommy up.

Tommy has no idea what he's doing. He's sound asleep and he thinks I'm someone else.

But then Alex started to wonder if Tommy really *was* asleep. His breathing seemed different, softer and more urgent. Alex could feel it like tiny breezes blowing across the right shoulder of his black T-shirt.

Minutes ticked by, but they felt like agonizing hours to Alex. He was immobilized with a wild sense of fear and anticipation. Every nerve in his body was flickering with electricity. Alex could almost see the energy in the dark—vivid blue and white flashes, glowing and zooming around the room like a dance troupe of fireflies.

Each time Tommy exhaled, the tip of his index finger would lightly touch Alex's skin, landing dangerously on his stomach. Alex closed his eyes and tried to concentrate on the lyrics in his mind, imagining Emily Haines singing them in his ear. He tried to think about anything that might make his hard-on go away.

He panicked a little, feeling paranoid. *What if this is a trap? What if Tommy is testing me? He'll tell everyone that I'm...*

Tommy shifted a little, still claiming sleep. His hand moved, drifting slightly downward from Alex's stomach to the front of his boxers. Alex held his breath, terrified to move. Tommy's hand was still, barely touching Alex, but it was close enough to create an intense feeling of pleasure soaring through Alex. He pushed his hips forward a little, inviting Tommy to take the moment further.

Alex was consumed by desire. A full-throttle rush was causing the lower half of his body to tremble. His teeth began to chatter.

Then, the realization that what he was doing felt unmistakably *right*.

It was at that pivotal moment that everything in Alex's searching mind unraveled and revealed itself in breathtaking clarity—a glorious feeling of surprise. Every thought and desire previously misunderstood, cleverly denied or rationalized, surfaced and bloomed in his mind. Trepidations that had traveled in his mind and heart since he was twelve were now greeted with the same unequivocal answer and explanation. The covert thoughts were set free, each carrying the potential destiny to forever change the world.

Alex smiled to himself; the realization of it was nearly strong enough to light up the entire bedroom.

I like men. I'm gay.

Alex wondered if Tommy was gay, too. *He can't be. He likes girls. He's the friggin' wingback on the football team.*

To answer the questions playing hopscotch in Alex's mind, Tommy lifted his head a little and whispered, "Don't tell anyone, Alex." The words showered down on the right side of Alex's face and trickled into his ear like warm drops of summer rain.

Alex swallowed, fearing he'd lost his ability to speak. His voice was a strained whisper when he responded, "I won't, Tommy."

Tommy lowered his head, placing the side of his face against Alex's. In unison, they closed their eyes, both physically overwhelmed by their lust and intrigue. "Can I touch you?" Tommy's voice tiptoed across Alex's skin.

Alex rolled over onto his back. "Yes," he breathed.

Tommy slid his fingers into the opening in the front of Alex's boxers. Alex shuddered, groping under the sheets, reaching for Tommy and the front of his briefs. Tommy moaned a little as Alex's hand made contact with his hot skin.

The two boys looked into each other's eyes as they caressed, fondled, and explored. It was a mirrored image, as both of them felt a simultaneous surge leaving them shaking with a shared comfort and camaraderie. As their lips caught fire by the single breath floating between their anxious mouths, their melting stares seared away inhibitions. They caught their first glimpse of a rawness and primal power they had never felt in themselves. In each other's eyes, they saw the arch of a bridge and they walked across, hand in hand, leaving the land of innocence and facing the undiscovered territory of adulthood.

For Alex, it would become a place he'd try to return to for the rest of his life.

❖

It had been Tommy's idea to spend the night. Alex wasn't surprised by the suggestion. In the few weeks Alex had worked the cash register at the Freemans' hole-in-the-wall pizzeria, he and Tommy had become close friends. They'd known each other for nearly twelve years but had rarely spoken.

In truth, they had very little in common. The pizzeria united them, an inevitable bond forming as their conversations evolved from mozzarella cheese and its origin to what life would be like once they graduated next year.

Tommy's world consisted of football, adulation from eager young women, and testosterone-fueled conversations in the hallway at school with hormonal buddies who leered lovingly at every pair of breasts passing them by. Although Alex was agile, athletics were not his interest. He preferred comic books, sci-fi novels, horror films, and skateboards. He didn't like to be part of the crowd, preferring to stand back and observe.

It became evident to Alex that Tommy was far more intellectual than his persona at school suggested. They started talking about religion, politics, and heated topics like the death penalty. Alex found himself looking forward to the nights he'd work with Tommy, even changing his schedule to afford them more time together. Alex wanted Tommy to feel important. He listened attentively to his words. Tommy loved to be venerated, and so Alex poured devotion on him.

Although Alex would never admit it, his conversations with Tommy and their body language were becoming increasingly more flirtatious and suggestive. The comfortable, warm giddiness Alex felt was spawned by Tommy's obvious desire to be in his presence. Alex had never felt such a strong bond with another man, not even his father.

Tommy's father was Boyd Freeman, whose deep Southern roots seemed to tangle around everything he did and said. He was a short, balding fellow who wore large, round glasses and had been cursed with a tremendous overbite. Boyd's given name had long ago been substituted with a cruel but sticking term of affection: Bunny. Like most things that truly bothered him, Boyd—or Bunny—shrugged off the name with a wink, a smile, and a tender and sheepish, "Y'all know that's not my name."

It seemed to Alex that Bunny's words for his only son were always thick with expectations. Alex wondered if Tommy represented the type of person Bunny would never be: athletic, charismatic, beautiful. The weight of perfection seemed to rest on Tommy's broad shoulders.

Alex watched Tommy work tirelessly in the kitchen of his father's restaurant, hunching over a stainless steel counter, kneading and forming perfectly round pizza crusts. From where he stood behind the register, Alex caught himself stealing glances at Tommy, noticing the way Tommy's fingers tightened when he massaged the dough, spreading it across a pizza pan, and how he smoothed it out around the curved edges of the metal plate.

It made Alex ache to be touched.

On the twelfth night they worked together, Alex started to wonder what it would be like to be touched by Tommy. He tried shutting the thought out, closing his eyes and erasing the imagined moment from his mind.

Tommy and Alex's friendship had shifted on the last Saturday in June. The hour was late—nearly closing time. Tommy's older sister, Sue Ellen, was on her cell phone, sitting in a booth in the empty dining room. Her congested laughter sprayed through the humid air. "You fucking kill me!" she howled, not losing count of the wad of bills she'd pulled from the front pocket of her apron. Although she'd put on a little weight in the two years since graduating from high school, Sue Ellen still knew how to earn big tips. Alex assumed the power she held was in her walk. Night after night, she sauntered through the restaurant like a cat, slinking around the corners of the place and rubbing up against the male customers. Sue Ellen did this so effortlessly, Alex felt awed. Often, he'd watch her from behind the front counter, waiting for her to pounce.

The Georgia summer air was thick and murky, even at night. The kitchen was unusually hot. Alex stood in the doorway, his back to the register and dining room, focusing on the beads of sweat forming around Tommy's temples. He liked the way Tommy's T-shirt clung to the small of his back. A tiny pool of perspiration had formed just above the waistband of his Bermuda shorts.

Alex licked his lips, ready to say something clever. But Tommy's words derailed his train of thought. "My sister thinks you're hot."

Alex cringed. "Your sister isn't my type."

Tommy laughed a little. Using his thumb and index finger, he flicked his right wrist, sliding thin slices of pepperoni onto the tops of two pizzas as if they were miniature Frisbees. The movement was quick and precise, almost automatic. Alex was mesmerized, his eyes locked on Tommy's hand. "My sister thinks she's everybody's type."

Alex tried to laugh but it caught it in his throat. "I thought she was dating Hunter."

"Dating?" Tommy laughed again, for both of them. "That's putting it nicely. I heard she gave Hunter a bad case of crabs."

Alex's cheeks flushed with guilt. He knew exactly who'd started that rumor. Jillian had done it out of spite. "Yeah, I heard about that."

Tommy moved closer to Alex and their arms touched. "Between you and me," he whispered, "my sister gets what she deserves. My dad spoils her like crazy."

"I don't know why he does," Alex replied, as if on cue. "Everyone can see you're the smart one in the family."

Tommy grinned and shot a look at him. It swam inside Alex's belly, warming him like the sips of Armenian whiskey he occasionally stole from the bottle his mother stashed behind the washing machine. "You don't have to say stuff like that," Tommy said.

Alex looked away, to the burning glow of a neon sign above the cash register. "Well, it's true."

Tommy stepped forward and Alex felt scared, unsure. "Hey," Tommy said with a sudden rush of excitement. "What are you doing tonight?"

"Same thing I do every night. Watch too much television or read comics."

"You don't have any plans with Jillian?"

"No." Alex looked down at the floor, to the black and white checkered linoleum tile. He'd been neglecting Jillian lately and he felt bad about it. "Not tonight. I think she's busy."

"I don't blame you, Alex." Tommy's words made Alex look up. He waited for clarification. "I wouldn't go out with a girl like Sue Ellen either. Not when I had a girl like Jillian. Now, she is *hot*."

"Me and Jillian are just friends."

Tommy tossed him a look. "You're shitting me, right?"

"No. There's nothing going on between us."

"Man, why not? Half of the school thinks you're boning her."

Alex shrugged his shoulders, battling an onslaught of unexplainable sadness. "Well," he answered, "I'm not."

Tommy moved closer, playfully tugged on the loose strings of Alex's white apron. "No plans tonight, huh?"

Alex's mood brightened. He shifted nervously in his black and white Converse. "Nothing special."

Tommy turned back to his pizzas on the shiny silver counter. He flicked a few more slices of pepperoni and asked casually, "You want some company?"

JILLIAN

In Jillian's oversized sunken living room, Alex looked down at what was sitting on top of the nicked wooden coffee table. "Backgammon?" he asked her. "We're playing backgammon on a Friday night? We've reached an all-time low, Jilli."

She reached up and pulled Alex down to the floor where she sat. "You got any better ideas?"

Alex pulled off his shoes. He crossed his legs, Indian-style, scooting across the worn-thin carpet and positioning himself on the opposite side of the coffee table from Jillian. "Plenty, but most of them are illegal."

Jillian grinned with hope, recognizing flashes of Alex's usual self. "Those will have to wait until our senior year officially begins in August. Tonight, you and I are playing *Nardi*." She kicked off her new sandals, the ones with white straps and pink daisies.

Alex gave her a strange look. His face was illuminated with the warm glow from the scented candles flickering around the sunken room. "*Nardi*? You've been spending too much time with my mother."

Jillian laughed a little and said, "Secretly, she hopes you and I will get married."

Alex flashed a smile. "She'll adopt you if you keep learning to speak Armenian."

"For some reason, it comes easy to me. How come *you* never speak it?"

Alex ran a hand through his dark, unruly hair and said, "People already think I look like a terrorist."

"Only because they're lame."

"Why bother speaking it? No one understands it. Especially my father."

"Yeah…but, still…it's a part of who you are."

"I'm only *half* Armenian," he reminded her. "My dad's a dumb redneck."

"I think it's a beautiful language, Alex. I love to listen to your mom speak when I'm—"

Alex shifted the conversation. "You've really gone all out tonight," he marveled, gesturing to the bottles of ice-cold Wild Cherry Pepsis, the green Tupperware bowl of potato chips, the store-bought plastic container of French onion dip, and the bag of pink and white marshmallows.

"I feel like we haven't spent much time together this week," she said.

Alex leaned back, resting his spine against the edge of the tattered olive green sofa behind him. "Is this a guilt trip?"

Jillian pushed the bowl of chips toward him. "No special occasion. I had time on my hands."

Alex sighed. "Is the parental unit still at work?"

"Whoring herself around Applebee's like an amateur call girl."

He grabbed a potato chip. Jillian watched as it moved toward his mouth. He ate it and wiped his hand on the leg of his black shorts. "I'm lucky I had tonight off."

Jillian leaned forward a little, confused. "Tommy said you

haven't been to work since last Saturday. He said you missed three of your shifts."

Tension filled Alex's posture. "You talked to Tommy?"

Alex's eyes narrowed and his cheeks flushed when he said Tommy's name.

Did they have a fight? "Last night," Jillian felt the need to explain. "I called there because I thought you were working late or something. He answered the phone and I grilled him."

Alex's answer was quick. "I was home last night. I thought I texted you."

Jillian reached for a pack of cigarettes sitting next to a giant seashell ashtray. "I figured you had to be working, otherwise you'd have been here."

"Was I supposed to be?"

The way he was so dismissive and irritated made Jillian want to throttle him. Instead, she lit her cigarette, took a short drag, and exhaled. "I waited and waited."

Alex's eyebrows shot up. "Your period?"

She felt exasperation seep into her words. "My birthday."

He lowered his head, his eyes. "Oh…fuck."

"That's right, Alex. I'm legal now. Eighteen with no future."

"This *is* a guilt trip."

"No. It's not. Although you deserve one."

He looked her in the eyes. "I do. I do."

She pulled herself up to her knees, the back of her heels holding the majority of her weight. "Make it up to me."

"I already told you, we're too good of friends. We can't sleep together."

Jillian replied, with a laugh and a quick shake of her head, flicking her honey-colored ponytail, "Yeah, like that would ever happen."

Alex folded his arms across his chest, barely covering the name of a famous comic book company. "What price do I have to pay?"

Jillian flicked her ashes. "Tell me why you weren't here last night. How come you've missed work all week?"

"I was right. You're working for my mother now."

"Why are you being so cryptic?"

"Why are you using big words?"

"I'm trying to make up for the fact I was held back in the fourth grade. I'm wiser than my peers, Alex."

"So you're a year older than everyone. Who gives a shit?"

"I'll be almost nineteen when I graduate next year."

"You'll still be neurotic and uptight, so I don't see what you're worried about."

She pointed at him. "You're changing the subject... *again.*"

He glanced at Jillian's third grade picture sitting in a gold frame on a lamp table. Jillian breathed deep, noticing how beautiful and smooth Alex's skin looked in the candlelight. "You said it was a habit of mine. A bad one."

She wasn't about to let him off the hook so easily. "Not one I like."

His hand went back into the chip bowl. "So, now there are conditions on our friendship?"

"Stop being a tease and tell me what's going on with you. You owe me that much."

Alex seemed spellbound by the flickering wick of a candle. "What's that smell?"

"The candles. They're scented."

He sniffed again. "What flavor?"

"Cotton candy. I bought 'em at one of those dollar stores."

"It smells like a carnival in here."

"I use them to mask the stench of bullshit permeating the air."

He reached for the plastic bag of marshmallows, opened it with his teeth. "There you go again. More big words."

"I'm trying not to swear so much."

He offered her a pink marshmallow. "I'm trying to avoid the subject."

She took the marshmallow from him and tossed it at his head. "You do it so well."

"I've just had a lot on my mind lately."

"Care to share?"

Alex opened a bottle of Wild Cherry Pepsi. "Not really."

"Should I be offended?"

"It has nothing to do with you."

"Well, whatever's going on, I hope it's worth it."

He took a moment and said, "I'm sorry about last night."

More ashes hit the bottom of the seashell ashtray. "It's no big deal. I enjoyed spending my birthday alone."

He looked at the candle again, as if he were finding solace in the blue and orange flame. "I would love to talk to you about this—"

She tried to burn a hole in him with her eyes. "Then why don't you?"

"I will, Jilli. When I'm ready."

"If you were a girl, I'd swear you were pregnant."

He looked at his best friend. She pulled back a little, slightly startled by the desperation in his eyes. "I need some time."

She felt sadness well up in her throat. "Away from me?"

Alex sighed. "Jilli, I'm not your boyfriend. Sooner or later—"

"If you're about to tell me you and I will eventually grow old and drift apart, I don't want to hear it."

"Fine."

"I invited you over to spend some time with you. You know I'm not very domestic, thanks to my freak maternal accident of a mother, so you can see…I've gone through a lot of trouble here."

"I apologize."

"Thank you."

"It's the least I can do."

"I appreciate that. I only wish I knew what you were apologizing for."

"I've been a complete jerk to you."

She exhaled again and a thin cloud of smoke circled around them. "You're forgiven."

Alex smiled and his dimples glowed. "So quickly?"

Jillian stubbed out her cigarette. "You're my only friend in the entire world. I can't afford to hold grudges."

"I will make this up to you."

"Yes, you will. You'll start by letting me win a few games of backgammon." She took a breath before correcting herself. "*Nardi.*"

July/Hulis

ALEX

Tommy and Alex were alone. A week had passed, and it was now July. Outside, fireworks exploded, ripping across the summer night sky like misfired hopes. Inside Alex's bedroom, they were in bed, face-to-face and bare-chested. Emily Haines's voice bled from a stereo in a dark corner of the room. Her words seem to crawl down the white walls and somersault across the wooden floors. A slice of sweat poured down the middle of Tommy's bare chest and Alex traced its path with his fingertip, humming the melody tickling his ears. "It's hot," Tommy breathed.

"It's an old house," Alex offered. "My dad put central air and heat in last winter. The thing's never worked right."

Tommy leaned forward and his lips brushed against Alex's as if they were exchanging a secret. Alex closed his eyes, falling into a deep sense of rapture. "I wish it could be like this all the time," he dreamed aloud.

"Well, it can't be," Tommy said, his words cutting through their shared reverie in the dark.

Alex's body tightened. A sharp pang punched him in the lungs. "What do you mean?"

"We have to be real about this."

Alex swallowed, overwhelmed by the sweet smell of Tommy's body. "Why?"

"School starts next month."

"And?" Alex prompted, searching for something in Tommy's eyes.

"Summer will be over soon."

Alex tried to shrug off the impending sense of doom he felt creeping underneath the door of his bedroom. "Is that what we are, Tommy? Are we a season?"

Tommy rubbed his eyes with the back of his hand. "You avoided me for almost a week."

"I was kinda freaked out, you know."

"I know."

"I've never done anything like this before."

Tommy's smile seemed awkward. "No one's forcing you."

"I'm not saying I don't like it."

Tommy breathed in deep, pressed his back against the bedroom wall. "What *are* you saying?"

"I never knew about you."

"What's there to know?"

"I thought you were just like everybody else. I never knew—"

"What?" Tommy's frustration muted Alex for a moment.

"How beautiful you were."

They fell silent for a moment, hypnotized by the whistling booms flooding their world in the distance. Tommy closed his eyes, as if lulled by the sounds and heavy heat of summer. Alex watched him, studying his features. He reached up and touched one of Tommy's dark blond curls. Tommy sighed and his stomach muscles tensed. "Everything feels different now," Tommy revealed, his eyes still shut.

"Because of what we've done?" Alex felt fear rising in his throat. "No one has to know."

Tommy's eyes opened and the liquid anger in them scorched Alex's skin. "They can't know. Not ever. I'm trying to get a football scholarship, Alex. It's my way out of here."

"I won't say anything."

"Well, if you do, I'll deny it."

Alex curled his toes as he felt heat and anger infiltrate his veins. He looked out of the bedroom window, where strobes of red, white, and blue lit up the town of Harmonville like a throbbing flashbulb. "What are you so scared of?"

"The same thing you are," Tommy shot back. "You didn't talk to me for a week."

"I didn't know you were angry." Alex reached for Tommy's hand. He held it in his own.

Tommy wove his fingers through Alex's. "I thought you were going to tell someone."

"Like who?"

"I don't know. Maybe Jillian. Or my dad."

"Why would I tell your dad?"

"Just don't, Alex."

Their hands separated and Alex pulled away, rolled over on to his back. He stared up at the ceiling, secretly hoping a firework would land on the roof of the house and burn the thing to the ground.

JILLIAN

The answer was right in front of her. Jillian stood, peering through the fence and wondering if she'd known the truth all along.

There'd been signs before, moments she'd overlooked or ignored.

Maybe on purpose.

But, now, it was as clear as day. She saw it with her own eyes.

Jillian slid her fingers through the chain links and pressed the cool metal against her palms. Alex had no idea she was there and watching. And she was so close to him. He was oblivious to everything, except for the dark-haired man on the diving board above them.

Jillian had cut through the park at the last moment, hoping to stumble across the old man selling snow cones. He pushed his freezer of crushed ice around the duck pond day after God-awful day. The portable cart squeaked and wobbled because of a rusted, crooked wheel. Jillian wondered why the half-blind bastard never fixed the damn thing. What did she care? As long as he kept selling those incredible paper cones of blue raspberry ice, nothing else mattered.

Except for the fact Alex was gay.

She spotted him at once, recognizing her best friend from yards away. She moved closer to the fence, intrigued. She kept her eyes on him, on his expressions. His body tensed and relaxed in the sun.

The neighborhood swimming pool was not very crowded, despite the scorching heat. A chubby female lifeguard sat high on a white wooden perch beneath a banana yellow umbrella. Jillian wondered if the sunburned girl was half-asleep, if her eyes were closed behind her oversized sunglasses, if she realized how unflattering her too-tight red swimsuit was.

In a white T-shirt and plaid shorts, Alex sat at the edge of the swimming pool like a patient lover waiting for his soul mate to return. His feet were in the water and the chlorinated liquid kept kissing his kneecaps. His eyes were lifted up, toward the sky. He licked his lips with anticipation, as if waiting to devour someone alive.

The stranger on the diving board shifted his body, prepared to jump. He was tall and strong. His wavy dark hair was wet and slicked back. His red and white Hawaiian print swim trunks clung to his body, fitting snug around his crotch.

Jillian noticed Alex's eyes. She followed his stare to the bare skin of the diver. She recognized the shine of lust in his eyes, the flash of desire. At once, Jillian let go of the chain links and stepped back away from the fence as if she'd been burned.

She knew Alex's secret. It had nothing to do with her.

She thought about scrounging in her purse for the dollar-fifty admission to get inside the pool. She wanted to sit next to her best friend, kick her sandals off and slip her feet into the water next to his. She wanted to hold his hand or wrap her arm around his shoulders and whisper in his ear, "You have excellent taste. He's beautiful."

Instead, she turned and walked away.

Jillian moved deeper into the park. She fought the urge to cry, mostly because it felt like such a ridiculous thing to do. She walked until she found the playground. Except for an Asian woman sitting on a bench reading a romance novel, Jillian was alone.

She kicked off her sandals and held them in her hand. She went to the swings and slid her hips inside an empty seat. Slowly, she pumped her feet back and forth until she reached the highest point possible, swinging high above the pit of sand beneath her. She clung to the chained ropes. They squeaked as she moved her legs faster and harder. Each time she lifted up to the sky, she imagined she was touching the clouds with her toes, walking across the expanse of summer blue. She was dancing away from Harmonville and into a world of neon lights and skyscrapers. There, she lived in floor-length black dresses and diamonds, sipping occasionally from an always-present cocktail glass and charming a roomful of strangers with just the sound of her laughter.

ALEX

On impulse, Alex followed the dark-haired stranger into the cavelike locker room. The place smelled of mold and chlorine. The cinder-block walls were damp with humidity, sweating from the inside out.

Alex turned the corner just in time to witness the stranger dip beneath the hot spray of a showerhead. Alex allowed his eyes to trail over the tan skin of the man who was at least twice his age. He was probably someone's father, some important executive of some important company there for a midday workout.

Alex stood as close as possible to the row of lockers, hoping his presence would remain unnoticed.

For a moment, he imagined what would happen if he stepped into the open stall with the beautiful man. Would they kiss? Would he let Alex touch him?

What if he's straight? He probably is. Wait. He doesn't have a wedding ring on.

With his back to Alex, the man slid his thumbs between his skin and the waistband of his red and white Aloha shorts and slowly began to lower them. The white flesh of his bare ass caused Alex to stop breathing for a moment. When he exhaled, his front pocket vibrated and his favorite Metric song blared out, revealing his voyeuristic perch.

The stranger turned over his bare shoulder and found Alex's eyes in the locker room. He lowered his gaze then, washing over Alex from head to toe, resting his stare for a moment on the front of Alex's plaid shorts, the obvious hard-on. He grinned a little and said, "Maybe you should get that," with an index finger pointed at the front of Alex's shorts.

Alex felt his face fume with humiliation. He slipped his hand into his pocket, pulled out his cell phone, and answered it. "Hello?"

His mother was on the other line, asking him questions in Armenian. He couldn't focus on her words.

"Slow down," he said with more firmness than he wanted to. "I don't understand you. Speak English, please."

Immediately, he knew he'd hurt her feelings. He could hear the tears rising in her voice, in her broken English. She tried to swallow them away, shove them out of her words, but it was no use.

Alex looked at the stranger and held his stare as the last glimmer of longing slid from his expression. "I'm on my way home," he promised his mother and ended the call.

The stranger was done with his shower and was toweling himself dry. Alex moved to leave, but the man's voice stopped him. "How old *are* you?" he asked, with a grin.

"Eighteen," Alex lied. He tried to hide the hope from revealing itself in his voice. He didn't want the stranger to know how lonely he was, how much he wanted to be with someone—not just to fool around with, like how it was with Tommy—but a real relationship. Nothing too serious, though.

The man again gave him the once-over, drinking him in and deciding, with a few shakes of his head, it wasn't going to happen. "You're just a kid," he said. "Come back in a couple of years. Then…we'll talk."

Alex nodded and tucked his cell phone back into his pocket. He turned away from the stranger and headed toward the exit.

JILLIAN

"Why didn't you just tell me?" Jillian asked two days later.

"I *did* just tell you," Alex responded, walking ahead of her.

Jillian almost had to run to catch up with him. "Why are you making me chase you?"

"I'm not," he huffed.

"Well, can we slow down, then? It's nine hundred degrees out here."

They were directly in the middle of their journey, two blocks away from Jillian's house and two blocks left to go before they reached Alex's. He crossed the quiet, narrow street and Jillian scrambled to keep up, nearly sliding across the hot asphalt in her pink and white daisy sandals. "I wanna get home," Alex explained.

Jillian half sprinted across the Killingers' front lawn as Alex hurried down the sidewalk next to her. "You're afraid to look at me, Alex Bainbridge."

"What if I am?"

"For God's sake, I'm your best friend. I don't care if you like men."

Alex whipped around and faced her. "Can you try not to shout it to the neighborhood?"

Jillian stared at him, and her own hurt feelings were reflected back at her. The tinge of rage in his eyes stung the center of her heart. "Why are you so angry?" she asked.

He folded his arms across his chest and clenched his fists. "I'm not."

She nodded, wiped at the corners of her eyes. She looked at the back of her hand. It was smeared with cheap eyeliner. "Yes, you are. And I have no idea why."

Alex turned away, looking down the street. Tears filled his eyes, surprising them both. "Look, it was really hard to tell you."

"I know that."

His voice cracked as he struggled to control his emotions. "This whole thing's been messing with my head for weeks now. Maybe even longer and I didn't realize it."

"But I'm your best friend," she reminded him. "And I love you…no matter what."

Jillian reached out and touched his face. He tried to pull away at first, but gave in and welcomed her palm against his cheek. "I love you, too," he offered back.

Jillian bit her bottom lip to contain her excitement. "Am I the first person you told?"

"Jillian, you're the *only* person I've told."

"This is un-fucking-believable. It makes me love you even more. I'm serious."

He lowered his voice. "Because I'm gay?"

She reached for his hands and squeezed them against her own. "Do you realize how close you and I are, right now at this moment? This is shit we'll remember for the rest of our lives."

His hands slipped out of hers. "If I live that long," he said.

Jillian pulled him into her arms, hugged him, and made a promise. "I won't breathe a word of this to anyone."

"If you do," he whispered back, "you know what could happen to me."

"Say no more."

He pulled away from her. "Someone told me half the school thinks I'm boning down on you."

She grinned. "No offense, but I wish you were."

He shoved his hands into his pockets and lowered his eyes to the edge of the curb. "Don't tell me you have feelings for me, Jilli."

"I do, but not like *that*."

He started to walk again and Jillian followed his cue. Their pace was slower now, less urgent. "Explain," he prompted her.

"You have no idea what it means, that you trust me enough to bare your soul. But I have to tell you…I'm really happy these dumbasses think you and I are having hot sex."

"Dare I ask why?"

Jillian took a quick breath before she spoke. "Because you're definitely the coolest guy in this awful town."

"There's lots of cool guys in Harmonville."

"Are you speaking from experience?"

He shrugged and laughed. "Maybe."

She gasped. "You son of a bitch. You're having sex and I'm still the Virgin Queen? What's up with that?"

They reached the bottom of his driveway. Jillian glanced up at the old wooden front porch. For a quick second, the pale amber haze of the porch light held her attention. *Strange*, she thought. *Why would the light be on during the day?*

"I wouldn't exactly call it *sex*," Alex offered. "I think *experimenting* is more like it."

Jillian only half heard what Alex was saying. An overwhelming sense something was very wrong swirled beneath her skin and tiptoed down her spine. She shivered. She swallowed and tried to forget the wave of nervousness rolling inside her body. She attempted to laugh it off and made the smart-ass comment that Alex was expecting from her. "You're not giving blow jobs to strangers like Sue Ellen Freeman does every Friday night, are you?"

"No," he replied, "you're sort of warm, but he wasn't a stranger."

Jillian allowed herself to be distracted by Alex's words. The chill of concern instantly faded. "I'm sort of warm and he isn't a stranger?" Jillian's eyes widened with disgust. "Oh God," she said, scrunching up her nose as if she were on the verge of puking on the oil-stained cement. "Please don't tell me you let Bunny Freeman do dirty things to you. He's *old*."

Alex avoided her eyes at first. "I don't know if I can talk about it yet," he said. He held her gaze. "I really want to tell you everything, Jilli."

She reached for him, but her fingertips missed his arm. "Whenever you're ready," she said.

Jillian wondered if she and Alex saw the light at the same time. It wasn't the porch light causing the air in their lungs to pause. It was a dull glow seeping out from the frayed bottom lip of the garage door. It seemed like a beacon of some sort to Jillian, an SOS signal from another realm. Someone was messaging for help. Someone wanted them to see the light, open the door, and discover their dire situation.

Alex moved first, breaking their frozen stances. He walked up the driveway and Jillian followed, almost tripping in her sandals. She felt they were moving in slow motion, stepping through knee-high molasses to reach the garage door.

She watched as Alex's hand wrapped around the rusted handle, twisted and lifted the door. It creaked open and rolled upward. The sound and movement were like knives slashing at their souls. The light swam across their bodies and slipped inside Jillian's mouth when she screamed. She tasted the hot glare of the light beaming from the overhanging burning bulb in the garage and it caused her to choke on a second scream.

When Alex broke away from her, Jillian lifted both hands up toward him. He flew across the garage to the center of it where his mother's lifeless body dangled from a thick black rope.

Jillian felt her heart stop the second she watched her best friend wrap his arms around his mother's waist and beg her to come back to life.

As tears poured down Jillian's face, she knew it was already too late.

August/Ogostos

ALEX

After his mother hanged herself in the garage, Alex didn't say a word for a week. When he did speak, a few days after his mother's casket was lowered into the ground, his words were in his mother's native Armenian: *"Haskanum em."* His American father, whose rail-thin body often betrayed his quest for strength, repeated the words back to him in English. "I understand."

They were on the sagging front porch, heavy and swollen from the August heat. Alex stood, pressing his weight against the waist-high balustrade. His hands were wrapped around the edges of the chipped white wood, his knuckles scraped and bruised. He'd punched a wall at church, denounced his belief in God, and fallen into a self-imposed muteness.

He looked up. The sky reminded him of melting ice cream—a dish of drippy oranges and pinks, swirls of purples, and a beautiful, haunting blue.

His father was close by, down on one knee and holding a scrap of sandpaper in his left hand, bent over some old wooden relic he'd found that day on his garbage route.

Alex made eye contact with his father for the first time in seven days. "I understand *why* she did it, Dad."

Alex shoved his hands deep into the front pockets of his

faded jeans. He'd spilled a bite of meat loaf at dinner, leaving a splash of tomato sauce on the chest of his white T-shirt. He shifted nervously from one foot to the other, his big toes wiggling inside his black and white Converse. He felt excited, as if he were reveling in the aftermath of an epiphany—a discovery that had the power to change his life forever.

Alex turned back to the sky, and a thin tear slid from the corner of his eye, trickling down to the tip of his nose. "She was homesick," he said. "She wanted to go home, Dad."

His father's throat made a strangling sound, as if he were choking to get words out. "Alex, I would've taken her to Armenia. I could've…we would've gone to Alaverdi for a visit. I would've done *anything*." Alex thought his father sounded desperate. It wasn't what he wanted to hear. He stepped back, wiping his eyes with a flash of his hands.

Alex's words were short and choppy, fused with anger. "Dad, that's *not* what I'm talking about. She wanted to go home to *Chicago*. She hated Armenia…and so do I."

"Alex…" His father reached for him, crumpling the sand paper in his hand. His fingertips brushed against Alex's forearm. He pulled away quickly, as if scalded. The touch was like the firing of a starter pistol for Alex. He bounded off the porch, hoisting himself up and leaping over the balustrade. His shoes landed smack dab in the middle of a family of wilting marigolds, heaving beneath thick layers of humidity. From there, he was off and running.

The front of the house stood back at least twenty yards from the picturesque residential street they lived on. Alex's first impulse was to head toward the street, zip past the standing mailbox, and race to Jillian's house.

Or he could go to the swimming pool, stare at a stranger and hope one of them felt sorry enough to touch him. Instead, he ran toward the back of the house.

Alex nearly tripped over a tangled garden hose. He moved on, across the cement patio and the backyard. He flew past an old marble birdbath, a barbecue grill in desperate need of cleaning, cheap patio furniture fading in the sun. Beyond the house, the earth sloped down and led him into a forest. The twenty acres standing before him had become his personal terrain, a place he could explore and seek refuge in. The land was overgrown, populated with huge clusters of trees, knee-high weeds, wild dandelions that tickled his ankles, and thick red Georgia dirt dampened from humidity and the frequent summer storms.

Alex loved to run. He liked the feeling of going somewhere. He'd always been restless, even as a child. He'd been unable to sit in the seat of a shopping cart, couldn't be content sitting in a movie theater or a church or a doctor's office. He had to be on the move. Nothing displeased him more than being idle.

Alex felt bad for leaving his father on the porch, but he was overwhelmed. The house was suffocating with its choking grief and the sad look of pity in his father's eyes. Since the funeral, home had become an emotional prison. Alex had watched his father's soul disintegrate, as if someone were letting water out of a bathtub.

Down a slow, slow drain.

Alex ran with intensity. His thin, long arms jetted at his sides, punching the air, propelling him farther and farther away from the house and his father. His black and white sneakers pummeled the red dirt as he charged on, racing with the speed and prowess of a jaguar.

Alex zipped between the trunks of magnolia trees, peach trees, oaks, pines, and maples. By the time he reached the water's edge, his left side was aching and his heart was beating like a rapid-firing machine gun. He gulped in air, feeling it burst and explode in his throat like fireworks. On instinct, he started undressing. He kicked his shoes off, tossed his jeans to the ground, and flung his T-shirt onto a hovering branch.

Without a second thought, he dove into the lake, a hidden and secluded body of water shaped and curved like the waxing crescent of a moon. The water sent a sharp, electric shock through Alex's body. He welcomed the sensation, feeling his senses spring to life simultaneously and every nerve ending ache with alertness. He swam with the same precise, smooth and effortless animal grace he ran with.

It was exactly fifty-two yards to a small island. Nothing more than a patch of land, no larger than a living room. The island was home to a powerful burr oak tree, its only inhabitant. *Quercus macrocarpa*. Alex said the scientific name for the tree over and over in his mind like a mantra. He did this each time he swam to the island, paying homage to the tree, his shelter.

Alex made the swim in less than a minute. He emerged from the water, his bare feet sinking deep into the red clay dirt. *Indian soil* was what his grandfather had called it. It was messy and thick and stained everything it touched, including Alex's skin.

Alex collapsed at the base of the tree. He pressed his shoulder blades against the gray bark. The backs of his bare legs were gouged by discarded acorns. He closed his eyes, listening to the water lapping against the shallow shore.

"*Quercus macrocarpa*," he said aloud, announcing his arrival to the tiny island. In Alex's mind, the tree whispered back to him, "Everything's going to be all right." It was a soft voice, a woman's. His mother's?

"Mom?" The urgency in his voice surprised Alex. He hadn't cried. Through the whole ordeal—from finding her dead in the garage, to the phone calls to friends and family members, to editing the obituary for the newspaper, to picking out the blue dress for her to be buried in, to losing his temper and denying God in church—Alex hadn't shed a tear. The sadness rising in his throat made him angry, made him feel weak. He'd almost cried in front of his father on the porch when he realized why his mother had killed herself.

Like her, Alex secretly wished to leave Georgia and return to the Windy City. It wasn't that he hated Georgia. Atlanta was only thirty minutes to the north from Harmonville. He lived in a great house. Sure, it was old and needed countless repairs, but it was a comforting place. He felt safe there. He had a handful of friends, Jillian being the closest. His grades were decent. But there was this ache he felt right before he fell asleep at night. It was the desire for something larger than life, something that left him trembling with inspiration and answers to his inner questions, no matter how minute or fleeting they were. He wanted something more, but he couldn't describe what it was.

Alex had been in Georgia since he was six. Harmonville was definitely his home. But those yearly trips up north, to the Midwest, were what he lived for. The relatives, the traditions, the customs, and the overwhelming feeling of belonging and being loved. Alex knew it was this powerful feeling that prompted his mother to step onto an ice chest, drag a dirty rope across the floor of the garage and wrap it around her neck.

She wanted to go home.

Alex's eyes fluttered open and his dark, thick lashes brushed against his cheekbones. He glanced out, scanning the surface of the water, hoping to see his mother's face in the murky reflection. Defeated, Alex allowed his tears to fall. He sat on his island, braced against the trunk of the solid oak, and sobbed for the death of his mother. The sadness felt like waves, wild and angry. They crashed inside him. He released them, giving them to the lake, where they drifted away. His chest rose and fell with a pounding relentlessness as he felt a cave begin to form in the center of his soul. Gutted, Alex feared the empty space left behind would not fill again for years—if ever. It would leave him embittered and jaded and envious of those who even appeared happy. It would leave him motherless, seeking comfort and nurturing in a world he'd grown to despise in the last week.

As the sun dipped behind the earth, Alex fell asleep, lullabied by the gentle rhythm of the water and the tender embrace of the burr oak. In his dreams, he swam. His arms cut through the water like human scissors, his legs kicking and propelling him, faster and faster, all the way to Chicago.

But he wasn't alone. He felt a presence on his back, soft and warm, radiating. With his mother's arms wrapped around his neck, he guided her home, where she had known love.

Much like Alex used to imagine heaven to be, when he still believed in such a place.

JOHN

As usual, John smelled from a long day of work. A combination of red Georgia dirt and rotting garbage reeked from his pores. He'd grown immune to it, as most men do who collect trash for a living. His son, who had an overly sensitive sense of smell, often held his breath when John was close to him. Tonight was no exception. Alex turned away on the porch, said something in Armenian, and exhaled.

Was he about to cry? John wasn't sure, so he moved forward, taking a cautious step. He was terrified he might say the wrong thing or move too quickly, and Alex would return to his state of self-imposed silence.

John stared at the back of Alex's head and noticed his son had grown at least two inches since Christmas. The boy was the spitting image of his mother. The smooth, olive, sun-kissed skin. The full mouth frozen in a permanent pout. The deep-set eyes, dangerous and sorrowful. The wild mass of black hair, framing his sharp, defined features with thick, loopy curls. The thin body, long neck, and sharp nose. Their similar features were a reminder to John that his beautiful wife was gone. Every time he looked at Alex, he saw her. He felt his chest tighten—a gnawing throb pulsed in the middle of his back.

Dinner had been insufferable as the two men sat across

the table from each other, picking over lima beans and leftover meat loaf. No words were shared between them, only grief. The silence was agony for John, who ached for the sound of his wife's gentle laughter and her spurts of broken English. He looked at the blank stare in his son's dark eyes and was terrified Alex might not ever fully recover from finding his mother's body in the garage. He wanted to hold his child and comfort him, but it wasn't in John's nature. He wasn't a cold man, but he'd never known affection from his own father.

John needed sound, something to fill the heartbreaking silence engulfing their lives. He stood up from the dinner table, grabbed the heart-shaped wooden chair he'd brought home from work and dragged it out to the front porch, letting the legs bang against the screen door as he escaped the grief-stricken house. *Sand against wood.* It was a rough, grating noise, but it was loud enough to kill the quiet. John sanded the chair down, ridding it of a horrible lavender paint and revealing its original pale hue. Alex followed him outside, picking bits of meat loaf out of his teeth. He cleared his throat, as if to say something, but remained silent. Instead, his attention shifted up to the sky, as if he were searching for something lost or for a hidden message snaking in and around the slowly drifting summer clouds.

Finally, Alex spoke, his words cracked and dry. *"Haskanum em."* John froze at the Armenian words. His hand stopped an inch away from the wood. He tightened his grip on the sandpaper, felt the roughness pressing into the center of his palm. He stood slowly and said the words back to Alex in English.

John, still cautious, moved closer. The urge to embrace his son returned and John silently cursed himself for not following through with his instinct. Siran had been the nurturer. She was always hugging Alex, kissing his cheek, even holding his hand on occasion. John worried if he attempted to offer affection, the moment would seem forced and leave them both feeling awkward. It would be just another reminder of what they'd lost.

Alex shouted at him—something about Chicago—leapt over the porch railing, and started running.

Once his son was gone, John accepted defeat and sat down on the top step of the porch. He wiped a bead of sweat from his left temple with the back of his hand. He sighed and felt his shoulders droop a bit. There was nothing he could do where Alex was concerned. The only option was to wait and hope his emotional state improved with time.

John thought about his wife. What had she been thinking when she knotted the rope around her neck, tossed it over a wooden beam in the garage, and then lifted off like a misguided rocket to heaven? Had she any idea of the pain she'd cause? Did she even care?

John felt sweat drip between his shoulder blades. The days were becoming unbearably hot, suffocating. Another summer in Georgia would soon come to an end. A summer that was very different than the previous ones. Summer had always been Siran's favorite time of the year. She never minded the heat.

John glanced across the front lawn as the sprinkler system turned on with a gurgling sound. Water began to pirouette across the neatly trimmed grass, splattering in whimsical, transparent patterns. John sat, mesmerized for a moment by the effortless grace of the water. Suddenly, he stood up and moved across the lawn, water spraying the legs of his jeans, soaking into his shoes and socks. The feel of the cold liquid caused him to breathe sharply. It awakened him with a jolt, creating a sudden sense of alertness.

Without a second thought, John sat down on the front

lawn. The sprinklers jetted across him, shooting across his chest like bullets. An unexplained smile flashed across his face. This behavior was ridiculous. The neighbors—especially Mrs. Gregory next door—would surely think he'd lost his mind. It was an impulsive, spontaneous thing to do. As water splashed into his eyes and mouth, he felt himself sinking lower into the dirt.

John realized the moment was crucial. It reminded him of who he used to be: fun, wild, unpredictable. Wasn't that why Siran had fallen in love with him nineteen years ago in Chicago?

John lay down on the grass, grazing his fingers through the tips of the wet blades. He looked up to the sky and found faces and figures in the clouds coasting over his neighborhood. He felt a sense of calm, a surge of euphoria, an adrenaline rush. He closed his eyes, welcoming the water against his skin.

He recalled the first time he saw Siran. The two of them had come face-to-face on the steps of the Art Institute on Michigan Avenue. Since that afternoon, they'd rarely spent a day apart from each other.

Now John was sprawled across the front lawn, soaked to the bone and trying to drown the overflowing sorrow reverberating inside his soul. He closed his eyes and focused on the *whoosh* of the sprinklers, chugging and anxious. John hoped he'd hear his wife's voice, calling to him from somewhere in the middle of the cold water.

MARTHA

M artha wasn't sure if he was alive or dead. She first spotted him when she decided to take a break from unpacking. She walked down her driveway to the edge of the road, checked inside the curbside mailbox—it was empty. Turning back toward her new home, she glanced quickly across the quiet street. At once, his body caught her eyes. She peered harder, squinting and trying to get a better look at the figure on the lawn. She breathed deep, feeling a wave of contemplation rumble through her body. She'd never been an impulsive woman before, but she was curious.

Martha crossed the street.

She hated Georgia. She already regretted the move. Harmonville was not the same as Pittsburgh. She missed the rush of the crowds, the urgency in the faces of strangers, sandwiches at Primanti Brothers, the collapse of each day when the lights from the bridges floated across the surface of the merging rivers.

It was this feeling of hollow emptiness that was plaguing Martha when she approached the man in the grass. She was homesick and lonely. But she'd been both of those things long before she ever reached the state of Georgia.

He was wet, the stranger on the lawn. His undershirt was

stuck to his body like a second layer of white cotton skin. His jeans were worn through at the knees and his work boots were caked with red mud.

"Excuse me?" Martha said from her nervous position on the sidewalk, near the edge of the grass. "Hello?" He didn't respond, didn't move.

Martha inched closer. She welcomed the drops of water sliding between her toes and licking the edges of her white sandals. She nervously patted the back of her head, smoothing loose strands of her almost platinum-blond hair up toward her high ponytail.

Her husband Harley often chastised her, saying she dressed too young for her age. He said she was obsessed with looking glamorous, she lived in a fantasy world, she wanted life to be like a magazine. But Martha ignored him. Instead, she waited until he was locked inside his home office, grading papers or reading Kafka while listening to that ridiculous opera music. Then she would sit by a window—usually one facing the Pittsburgh skyline—and imagine her escape.

Over the years, Martha often thought about packing a bag, slipping out in the middle of the night, and disappearing to a seaside town—maybe a postcard place in Florida—and she'd start a new life, without Harley and his constant need to correct everything she said or did.

But now escape seemed impossible. In Pittsburgh, Martha could've dived into the sea of strangers and floated away with them, hopping a Greyhound bus headed for the ocean and the sun. Here—in a small town in Georgia—Harley would certainly know her every move. Here, she'd have to pretend she loved her husband, for the sake of appearances. He was, after all, the new English teacher at the high school. It wouldn't be long before everyone knew him—and his lovely wife, too.

The thin man on the lawn didn't look like Harley. No

paunch. No receding hairline. No permanent, arrogant smirk. No five o'clock shadow. Instead, Martha found herself captivated by the stranger. As the tips of her toes reached the side of his torso, she prayed silently he was indeed alive.

He must have sensed her presence. He cracked an eye open and it was so blue, Martha wondered if the sky had flipped upside down and crash-landed into his gaze. He licked his lips and opened his mouth as if he wanted to say something but the words got stuck in his throat. Thick strands of his salt-and-peppered hair were wet and stuck to his forehead.

Martha offered a smile and said, "You're alive."

The man lifted himself up and rested the strength of his body on his elbows. "My God," he whispered. "You look like...like...an angel."

In truth, his words were the gentlest and most sincere ever spoken to Martha. They were filled with awe and enchantment. They caught her by surprise and they danced in the humid air around her and they kissed her neck. It was no wonder that inside her body, Martha felt a shiny twinkling—a beautiful shimmer.

As if the city lights from Pittsburgh had somehow found their way back to her.

ROBBY

Robby knew his mother was unhappy. She'd been desperate for affection for as long as he could remember. She was always asking him for a hug or to sit closer to her. She hated being alone and she said so. "My days are lonely, Robby," she'd tell him after school. She held him so tight she pushed the air out of his lungs. "This house is too quiet for me. But when I go downtown, it's too loud."

That afternoon, Robby stood at the window inside his new bedroom and watched his mother cross the street and approach the man lying on his front lawn. She stood over his still body, and Robby's breath stuck in his throat. He swallowed a lump of fear, worrying their new neighbor might be dead. But within seconds, the guy was up and shaking her hand. He was practically tripping over his feet to talk to her.

After watching their giddy first meeting, Robby predicted his mother would have an affair before the summer was over, and leave her husband by Christmas.

If not sooner.

If I was married to Harley, I would have left him a long, long time ago.

Robby was no dummy. He knew his mother was hot. The

men who lived on their old block in Pittsburgh would stare at her like she was something they always wanted but knew they'd never have. They watched her like a kind of supernova lighting up their dark lives with her electric smile and white-blond hair. They opened doors for her. They tipped their hats. They wiped their dirty palms on their jeans whenever she was around. They smiled too much, laughed at their own jokes. And they waited. Just a few soft words from her would spin them out into a spiral of bliss. And it showed all over their love-struck faces.

That's what I want, Robby thought, staring through the glass. *I want to be love-struck.*

Like his mother, Robby felt alone in the world. "You're just a misfit," she told him when he was six after a playground bully had labeled him a "sissy" and punched him so his nose bled for nearly an hour. "You're a beautiful misfit…and you're all mine."

She took him home from school that day, made him a cup of Ovaltine, and stared at him for hours. Whenever he glanced up at her, she always looked like she was about to cry.

The word "sissy" followed Robby through the rest of his childhood. The playground became a battlefield and Robby was the eternal survivor. No matter how hard they hit him, he wouldn't cry. He wouldn't scream out for help or yell for a teacher. He took their punches and kicks and refused to let them know how much they hurt him. He wore his bruises and cuts with pride, brandishing them like badges of honor won by withstanding beating after beating.

He was seventeen now. The words were angrier and the fists were more violent. He couldn't escape the teasing, no matter how hard he tried. The locker room and P.E. class were the worst. The coaches would look the other way, and a couple would even chuckle when he was pummeled and taunted. Robby grew accustomed to it, until being beaten up became normal and routine.

Robby had become a moving target for the guys who hated him because they knew he was gay. The truth was Robby had never even kissed a guy before, let alone messed around with one. He knew he wasn't attracted to women, but men…they were still a mystery.

He knew he was the reason they had left Pittsburgh. Robby knew Harley blamed him for the move. "I guess we don't have a choice," he said looking down at the word "faggot" spray-painted in bright red on the sidewalk outside of their home one morning. "We have to leave."

Robby's father had gone inside, but his mother stayed outside with him. She held him and caressed his hair. "It's okay," she told him. "I've always hated Pittsburgh."

Later that night, Robby overheard a conversation that broke his heart. "You don't know what it's like, Martha," Harley said behind the closed bedroom door. "He's *my* stepson and everyone at school thinks he's a freak. You should see how the other teachers look at me."

"What do you want me to do, Harley? He's my son. There's nothing wrong with him."

That was two months ago, before they packed up their belongings, loaded boxes and furniture into a truck, and headed south to a little town called Harmonville—a place where Harley's dead grandfather had once spent a summer years ago and christened "a perfect place."

Robby's mother was now sitting next to a stranger on his front porch. She was laughing and tossing back her head, shielding her eyes from the setting sun.

Or maybe she didn't want the stranger to see the ache inside her soul.

He was mesmerized by her—the tall man in the wet clothes. He couldn't take his eyes off her. It seemed like he wanted to drink her laughter, sip it right out of her mouth.

Robby's eyes suddenly shifted. The dark-haired boy seemed to appear out of nowhere. He came from the side of the house and stood in the center of the lawn. He stared at the adults on the porch and shoved his hands into the back pockets of his jeans.

There was anger in his tense posture and a rebellious flair in the way he smashed the grass with each step he took. There was something in the way the boy stood that intrigued Robby, beckoning him like a secret invitation slid beneath his door. *Come here. You've been waiting for me.*

Robby couldn't move fast enough. He searched his unpacked room for a pair of flip-flops, fishing them out of an overstuffed duffel bag. He stepped into the shoes without realizing they didn't match. He collided with stacks of cardboard boxes covered with his nearly illegible scrawl in permanent marker.

He almost slid down the carpeted stairs, skipping the last few steps altogether. He leaped off the third to the last stair and landed in the marble-tiled foyer. He yanked the front door open and forced himself to stop and take a breath. Otherwise, his mother might freak out and think the house was on fire.

Robby crossed the street to the white house with the pale blue shutters. He slowed his pace when he reached the curb and almost turned back for home when he reached the driveway.

But then the boy with the wet dark hair turned and looked at Robby over his shoulder. Their eyes met. In that second, Robby knew nothing in his life would ever be the same. He felt his chest tighten, his pulse quicken. *He just took my breath away.*

Behind Robby, the August sun began its final descent and slipped beneath the horizon.

"Hey," the boy said. His voice was deeper than Robby expected. Tough, even. Like no one could mess with him.

"Hi," Robby replied, after finding the courage to look the beautiful boy in the eyes.

He pulled a hand out of his back pocket and offered it to Robby. "I'm Alex."

Robby placed his palm against Alex's and an invisible charge was lit. They shook. "I'm Robby."

Alex glanced down at Robby's chest, and it made Robby blush instantly. He could feel Alex's breath tickling his face. It was warm and smelled sweet. The baggy T-shirt Robby was wearing suddenly felt twenty sizes too big for him. "You like Metric?" Alex asked, tapping the letter "M" on Robby's concert T-shirt with a fingertip.

"They're the best band in the world." Robby beamed, still watching Alex's mouth. "I mean…other than Garbage, of course."

Alex glanced down and laughed a little. Robby was tempted to ask him what was so funny. As if he could read Robby's thoughts, he explained. "Your shoes. They're two different colors."

Robby looked down to his toes and wiggled them. "Black and blue," he noted, feeling embarrassment continue to tinge his cheeks.

"Black and blue," Alex repeated. "You just move here?"

Robby nodded. "Yesterday."

"Where from?"

"Pittsburgh."

"Wow," Alex breathed. "Why in the hell would you come *here*?"

"My stepdad. He made us move."

Alex cracked his knuckles and stretched. His T-shirt lifted up and Robby couldn't help but catch a quick glimpse of the tiny trail of dark hair on Alex's stomach. "Your stepdad sounds like a real dick, if you ask me," he said.

Robby couldn't help but smile. "You have no idea."

Alex leaned in close and their mouths were close enough to kiss. "I think I do know," he whispered.

Although Robby wanted to turn away out of shyness and his fear of the unknown, the intense euphoria shooting through his body gave him a shot of courage—enough bravery to take a leap of faith. "Yeah," he replied, without hiding the gleam of lust in his eyes, "I bet you do."

"Come on," Alex said, reflecting back the same desire in his smile. He tugged on the sleeve of Robby's shirt. "The summer isn't over yet."

September/September

JILLIAN

Jillian didn't want to like Robby LaMont. In fact, before she met him in person, she'd already decided he would replace Sue Ellen Freeman and become her new nemesis, her enemy *numero uno*. For the last few weeks, he was all Alex talked about. It was "Robby is so funny." And "Robby is so cool." And, finally, "Robby is so cute. I think I'm in love."

Jillian tried to sound happy for Alex during their few-and-far-between phone conversations. She wanted to sound convincing but was certain Alex saw right through her feigned insistence that "You met someone. Great. I'm really happy for you."

Jillian's mind was made up before Saturday afternoon at the Labor Day church bazaar, when she and Robby came face-to-face for the first time. Whenever their first meeting took place, Jillian wasn't planning on being an outright bitch, but she wasn't going to go out of her way to be nice to him, either. Obviously, he was trying to steal her best friend away from her. Did the boy even know who he was messing with? She was determined to make sure he received her message loud and clear.

Jillian was miserable and hot. The bazaar was crowded

and never-ending. Behind the church in a grassy area, twenty or so tables had been set up in the shape of a horseshoe. Each one offered an array of homemade crafts, bottled jams and pickled fruits, hand-woven baskets, and baked goods. In the near distance, the minister and his plump wife were having a low-level argument while flipping burgers and hot dogs on a grill. Jillian watched intently, secretly hoping the self-righteous woman would lose control, freak out, and make a hilarious spectacle out of herself.

Jillian stood behind a table selling red raffle tickets to anyone she could sucker into buying them. She collected dollar bills, taking them from sticky fingers and sliding them into the blue double-pocketed apron she wore around her hips. "Raffle tickets! Get your raffle tickets here!" she hollered.

Each time a car arrived or drove away, loose dust rose up from the gravel parking lot next to the church and drifted in Jillian's direction. She coughed, rubbed her eyes, and fanned the air, but there was no relief. The dirt was choking her to an early death.

Yet from where she stood, she could see everything and everyone. She noticed the fresh hickey on Sue Ellen Freeman's neck when she strutted by the ticket table in a miniskirt and tank top (two sizes too small for her, like always) and muttered, "Dirty bitch." Jillian replied with a wicked smile and the words "Fuck you very much, fat ass."

Tommy trailed behind his older sister. He offered Jillian a gentle wave. At once, she saw loneliness lingering deep in Tommy's eyes.

Jillian began to take great delight in her observations. Bunny Freeman was going bald and walked like he had a ginormous stick wedged up his ass. Hunter Killinger thought he owned the place when he walked in wearing fake sunglasses and way too much imposter cologne. His ridiculous wannabes followed him around like he was Jesus carrying a cross—especially that idiot Eric Lowe, whom Jillian suspected was suffering from an undiagnosed case of Tourette's Syndrome. Mrs. Gregory—the old bat who still believed the South won the Civil War—kept trying to push her gaudy macramé plant holders on everyone, even though the style hadn't been popular in decades. She was practically threatening people to buy them, blackmailing them with their own family secrets.

Jillian's eyes widened. Alex's father apparently already had a new girlfriend—a stunning woman with blond hair and a toothpaste-commercial smile. They giggled at each other, strolling through the bazaar and speaking silently with their eyes. But the beautiful woman stepped away from John Bainbridge and joined a dark-haired man Jillian assumed was the woman's husband.

Immediately, Jillian dove into a front pocket of her apron and whipped out her cell phone. She typed, "WTF? Is your dad having an affair with a blonde with a hot bod?" She was just about to press the Send button when the short husband suddenly appeared on the other side of the ticket table from her. He cleared his throat to make his presence known. Jillian glanced up and shoved her phone away, as if she'd been caught doing something wrong. She even felt her cheeks blush, and this pissed her off.

Who in the hell is this guy sneaking up on me like that? Wait…oh, shit…he's old…but he's kinda cute. Nah…forget it… he's too short.

"Hello," he said. His voice was smooth. It reminded Jillian of a man who hosted a call-in radio show her mother used to listen to religiously. "How much are the raffle tickets?"

Jillian refused to crack a smile. It was too humid to be polite. Besides, the guy was clearly an idiot if he had no idea his sexy wife was hot for Alex's dad. "One dollar each."

He reached for his wallet. "Does the money go to a good cause?"

"That depends," she answered with a half shrug. "Do you like cops?"

He grinned, and Jillian had to admit it: she liked his smile. He had nice teeth. And his eyes were gorgeous—blue and icy. "I like to keep them on my side," he said. He pulled out a five-dollar bill and handed it to her.

She glanced down at his hands, at the dark hairs on the back of his thick knuckles. He was holding something. As if he could sense her stare, he opened his palm and flattened it to reveal a black box with Chinese writing on it. A ceramic dragon sat on top of it.

"Have I intrigued you with this?" he asked. Jillian was suddenly aware the stranger was leaning across the table and his mouth was close enough to kiss. She noticed a spot on his chin where he'd probably cut himself shaving that morning. She breathed deep, swallowing the scent of him: a mixture of manly soap, aftershave, and sweat. Yes, he was old...old enough to be her father. But it was evident he wanted her in the way his eyes kept dropping to her chest and rising up again to study her mouth. He wanted her *bad*. Heavy desire slid over their skin like an invisible hot mist.

Although Jillian had next to zero experience with guys, this married man was coming on to her in a big way. She could tell. *But so can everyone else.* If she'd spent the last hour people-watching, she was certain someone in the crowd was watching them, too. Whoever this man was, the last thing she wanted was a nasty rumor to spread around town about the two of them. Enough rumors were already circulating about Jillian's mother and her new boyfriend of the week.

"Are you wondering what I'm holding in my hand?" he asked, as if he were daring her to undress right there in the middle of the bazaar, let him make love to her while everyone watched.

She licked her lips before she answered. "Do you mean right now? Or every night?"

He raised an eyebrow. "I'm impressed. You're quick-witted," he assessed, adding, "and terribly sexy as well."

"Okay," she said, shifting her gaze back to the charcoal black ceramic box resting in his hand. "I'll admit it. I'm curious. What is it?"

"It's a wish box," he explained. "It's Chinese. It's feng shui."

"Never heard of it before," she said.

"It's simple. You write down something you wish for and you put it in the box." As if to demonstrate, he reached two fingers around the dragon and lifted the lid. "The dragon will guard your wishes so they come true. Pretty cool, don't you think?"

He held the wish box out to her. She took it from him, noticing the flash she felt sear her body when their fingers touched briefly during the exchange. "Yes," she said, locking eyes with him. "Very cool."

He grinned and said, "I'm Harley." She watched his lips when he spoke. "Harley LaMont. And you are?"

"LaMont?" she repeated. "As in Robby's father?"

He looked perplexed. "Stepfather," he corrected her. "But I gave him my last name."

"That's very...*noble* of you."

"If I'm noble, you're *clever*."

"No," she said with a small laugh. "Just Jillian."

"Jillian," he echoed.

"Jillian Dambro," she said. She ripped off five raffle tickets from the roll and handed them to him. "And...I think I'm in your fifth period class this semester."

He let the tickets go. Jillian watched them glide down to the grass. They landed at his feet. He was wearing loafers.

Another strike against him.

Who in the hell wears loafers on a Saturday? During summer? What a dork. Damn...he needs to stop staring at me because he's turning me on.

"Come again?" Harley asked, stunned.

She leaned in and whispered in his ear. "You're my new English teacher."

"I'll be damned," he whispered back. "This is going to be a very tough year."

Jillian inhaled him again. She wanted to lick his skin, taste him. "For me or for you?"

"For both of us," he decided. She pulled away from him and glanced around to make sure no one had witnessed the obvious sexual attraction between them. "Not only am I your English teacher...but I'm a married man."

As if on cue, his wife appeared next to him and slid her arm through his, claiming what was hers. Her wedding ring grabbed a ray of September sunlight. "Who's this?" the woman asked, but the question was posed more to Jillian than to her husband.

"One of my new students," he offered. "Jillian, this is my wife. Martha." The way he said "Martha" made her name sound like a synonym for "buzz kill."

Jillian's smile vanished and no matter how hard she tried, it refused to return. "It's nice to meet you...Mrs. LaMont."

"Please...call me Martha," she said with a flash of her ultra-white teeth. "We just moved here. From Pittsburgh."

"Yes, I know," Jillian said. "Alex told me."

Her bright smile dimmed at the mention of Alex's name. "Oh," she stated flatly. "You know Alex?"

"He's my...best friend."

Martha LaMont's posture tightened as if a string was pulling her from above. "Then you must know my son."

Jillian put the wish box down on the ticket table and folded her arms across her chest. "I know of him. I just haven't met him yet," she said. "Alex seems to be keeping Robby all to himself these days."

The conversation was obviously making Martha uncomfortable. In Jillian's opinion, the gorgeous woman couldn't change the subject fast enough. "What a beautiful wish box," she marveled. "My husband bought one just like it at that table...over there. Honey, do you have yours with you?"

Harley's words seemed strained, irritated even. "It's already in the car, dear."

Martha patted the back of her head as if she were making sure a hair hadn't escaped from her high ponytail. "Well," she said, "I guess we should be going now."

"We just got here," Harley reminded her. He lowered his voice, but his jaw was tense. "You bugged me all morning about bringing you here."

Martha was flustered, nervous and embarrassed. Jillian felt very bad for the woman. She wanted to say something to her but couldn't decide on the right words to say.

Maybe something like, "Martha, your husband is an absolute pig and doesn't have a faithful bone in his short, pudgy body. So, let me take him off your hands...at least until I graduate."

Instead, all Jillian could muster was, "See you in class on Tuesday, Mr. LaMont."

He started to walk away with his hand placed on the small of Martha's back as if ushering her along, as if he couldn't get her to the car fast enough. He looked back over his shoulder at Jillian and devoured her with one quick sweep of his eyes over her body. "I'm looking forward to it," he said.

Jillian glanced around, and sure enough Sue Ellen was lurking around, stuffing her face with pink cotton candy. She shot Jillian an all-knowing look and Jillian flipped her off in response.

She picked up the wish box and held it up in the air, inspecting it from all angles.

My first wish, she thought, *is to get me the hell out of this town. And fast. Take me away, wish box. To a big city.*

She reached under the table and slipped the wish box into her purse. For some reason, Jillian felt an immense wave of guilt. Martha's sweet smile kept flashing in her mind. And the way Harley had been so firm with his wife was unsettling. *I haven't done anything wrong*, Jillian reminded herself. But, deep down, Jillian knew she wanted to. It was only a matter of time before she and Harley would find themselves alone.

And she feared what would happen when that moment came.

She thought about sneaking off to hide somewhere behind the church to have a cigarette, but with her luck, she knew she'd get caught. Sue Ellen would no doubt follow her just to snitch to the minister and his spatula-pointing wife.

Five o'clock needs to hurry up and get here because I'm done with this place.

When Jillian saw Alex and Robby walking through the bazaar together, the pang of envy she'd been feeling dissolved into a warm mixture of melancholy and endearment. There was no denying Alex and Robby were an adorable pair. The glances they shared and their matching grins told Jillian all she needed to know: it was serious.

Maybe it really *was* love.

The rage and pain holding Alex captive since the start of summer had subsided. In its place was an electric illumination, a neon aura pulsing with golden bliss. He was glowing when he walked up to the ticket table and said, almost breathless, "Jillian…this is Robby."

"Hey," she said, keeping the nonchalant expression on her face tight.

Robby was a couple of inches shorter than her. He was small and fragile-looking, like someone who needed to be taken care of and protected. He stood next to Alex, half-hiding behind him. He looked at Jillian with his big brown eyes, but only for a few seconds. "Hi," he said in a soft voice. He glanced up from his blue raspberry snow cone, smiled a little, and then lowered his eyes back to the ground. "Wow," he enthused. "You're really pretty."

"Thanks," she muttered, hoping he couldn't tell his compliment worked, cracking her tough exterior. He was a little too girly for her taste and she couldn't really understand what Alex saw in him, but he seemed like a cool guy. "What are you guys doing here?" she asked Alex.

He gave her a look. "Maybe I should ask you the same question. Since when did you become a Baptist?"

She grinned and almost laughed. "Since my mother bribed me. She said if I help out at this dumbass bazaar, she'll finally pay to get my car fixed once and for all."

Alex scanned the crowd. "Is she here?"

"Yeah," Jillian said. "Probably in somcone's backseat in the parking lot."

Robby laughed a little and Jillian glared at him. "Sorry," he muttered.

"What are you apologizing for?" she asked. "You haven't met my mother yet…but once you do…I'm sure you'll understand everything…why I'm such a bitch."

MARTHA

Martha knew what she had to do. When she suggested a school shopping trip to John, he eagerly agreed. She presented her idea as an opportunity to get to know Alex better. She knew John's son couldn't stand the sight of her. He was always looking at her with an unsettling expression combining judgment and disdain, reminding her constantly of Harley and his never-ending barrage of criticisms.

Harley's recent crusade was against Martha's weight. He insisted she'd put on at least ten pounds in the month they'd been living in Georgia. He accused her of sitting around all day and feeling sorry for herself, demanding she do her fair share around the house. He noticed the smudges on the windows, the crumbs on the kitchen counter, the footprints in the carpet, the hair in the bathtub, the wrinkles in his shirts. He appeared exasperated with her, tired of being forced to remind her about everything—the bills needing to be paid, items from the grocery store to pick up, errands to run. She forgot them all unless he told her what to do.

She always felt his eyes on her, assessing her, and secretly celebrating his discovery of each of her flaws. He watched her every bite during the few meals they shared until he stood up at the table last night and announced, "I've lost my appetite." She nodded and felt tears burning the back of her throat. He looked down at her, her plate, her body, and said, "Maybe I should start eating dinner in my office. That might be better for the both of us."

According to the scale in her bathroom, Martha had only put on two pounds since leaving Pittsburgh. She desperately wanted to point out to Harley he'd gained at least forty pounds during their nine-year marriage. Instead, she would keep her mouth shut and eat dinner alone or with Robby in the dimly lit dining room. Above her upstairs, Harley would blast his opera music while shoveling his meal down. Maybe, if Martha were lucky, Harley would choke.

❖

Martha longed for every second she was able to spend with John. In his company, she felt young and beautiful again. She felt like the seventeen-year-old girl who dreamed of becoming a professional dancer. He reminded her of a time when she felt invincible, when she was stepping off the train in Pittsburgh for her first time, her whole life ahead of her.

John made her laugh and listened to every word she spoke. He took her seriously and respected her, asked her often for her opinion. He engaged her in conversations. Sure, they weren't particularly deep and tended to center around life in Harmonville or interesting items he'd found on his garbage route, but she appreciated them.

And she noticed John carefully avoided the topic of her marriage.

Maybe he knows. Maybe he can tell how unhappy I am. That I stopped loving Harley years ago.

Martha couldn't deny she was attracted to John. She

thought about kissing him, fantasized about making love to him, wondered what it would feel like to have him deep inside her. But Martha knew she had to keep her burgeoning crush to herself. As long as their relationship consisted of friendly flirting and remained harmless, the situation was safe. Besides, she'd never allow them to cross that line. She'd never be unfaithful to her husband. She wasn't that kind of woman.

Sometimes when she looked into John's eyes, or he smiled at her, she'd remember the affairs Harley had. He'd begged for her forgiveness, swore it would never happen again. And she'd taken him back.

Twice.

Last month, she even agreed to leave Pittsburgh to avoid the shame of the scandal. After what he'd done to that poor girl—his own student. It was best to leave town before everyone found out, especially her son. Hadn't he already been through enough?

Martha wasn't a spiteful woman, but she recognized the opportunity to pay Harley back for every unkind word, every indiscretion. For every dinner she ate in silence and solitude. For his ridiculous punishments for being too lazy, too old, too fat.

She could sleep with John and serve her husband a hot dish of comeuppance at the same time. The thought of it all was very tempting.

If only she were a woman who wanted revenge.

On the afternoon she'd found John lying in the wet grass, Martha knew John's son didn't like her from the moment they made eye contact. At first, she couldn't figure out why. She was polite and smiled. Yet he refused to shake hands with her. Instead, he folded his arms across his chest and balled up his fists. He locked eyes with her, warning her silently to stay away. He was staunchly claiming his territory and making it clear, without speaking a word, that she wasn't welcome in his world.

Within days, Martha realized what her presence meant to him. He was a sharp kid and he'd immediately recognized the intense connection between her and his father. He was terrified she'd try to take his mother's place.

The idea was ridiculous, of course. Siran had just died a week ago, and Martha was married.

At the moment they first met, Martha had no idea about what Siran's suicide had done to their lives. She only knew this dark-haired teenager with the defiant smirk couldn't stand the sight of her.

Other than Harley, Martha was used to being well-liked by everyone she knew. Alex's immediate dislike of her caused her to ache inside.

The same could not be said for Alex's reaction to Robby. As Martha sat on the porch next to John, watching the first meeting between the boys, she knew she was witnessing the blossom of young love. The desire between Alex and Robby was obvious and powerful. The way they took a second too long to shake each other's hand, and kept stealing glances at each other, told her all she needed to know. Right before her eyes, her son illuminated from within and glowed with a new lust for life.

Since they'd met, Alex and Robby had barely spent a second apart from each other. Martha had recently wondered just how close the two boys had become. Were they intimate when no one was around? Were they sleeping together?

❖

"It's really none of your business," Alex answered when she asked him if he spoke Armenian. He had emerged from his bedroom, where he and Robby had been locked away doing homework. He pulled a package of cookies out of the pantry and fished two cans of soda out of the fridge. He softened his tone a little and said, "I don't mean to be rude to you, Mrs. LaMont."

She was standing in the Bainbridge kitchen, making lasagna. Her hands were covered with ricotta cheese and tomato sauce. John was still at work. She'd wanted to surprise him with a home-cooked meal. She still had to run back home and reheat a plate of leftovers for Harley before he came home from his second day of teaching English at the high school. "I was just curious," she said to Alex, smiling. "I've never met someone who spoke Armenian before."

"My mother spoke Armenian," he explained. "She was born there. But she met my father in Chicago. In front of the Art Institute." At every given opportunity, it seemed Alex would mention his mother, reasserting her memory. "I bet it was very romantic."

Martha went to the sink and turned on the faucet, rinsing off her hands. "And you?" she asked. "Where were you born?"

He shot her a look, tucked the package of cookies under his arm, and stacked the two soda cans together into a single tower. "In a hospital."

She let his words roll right off her back. "I was thinking… maybe I could take you shopping. You know…for school clothes…and supplies."

He sighed with solid irritation. "Why would you do that? You hardly even know me."

She folded her arms across her chest. "Who else is going to take you, Alex?"

He wouldn't hold her stare. He looked out the kitchen window. "Suit yourself."

He started to leave the room. She stopped him with her words. "You and my son have been spending a lot of time together."

He froze in his steps. Slowly, he turned back. "Yeah? So?"

"So…I'm happy…I mean, for the two of you…that you… found each other."

In other words, I know you're gay and you're probably having a relationship with my son. I'm trying to be a nice person, here. I'm trying to give you my blessing.

If Alex was nervous, he didn't let it show. "So are we," he replied. "*Very* happy."

Martha swallowed. She didn't want him to know he intimidated her. "It seems like the two of you get along really well," she said. "That the two of you like each other."

Alex took a step toward her and she backed up against the counter. "We're not sleeping together…yet…if that's what you're asking."

Martha bit her tongue, holding back the torrent of words she wanted to pelt him with.

Alex leaned in and whispered, "Robby wants to, but I'm insisting we *wait*."

Martha winced when she felt the cold aluminum of one of the soda cans gently graze against her arm. He was standing too close to her. She felt cornered, trapped.

"I suggest you do the same thing…with my father." He

disappeared then, back to his bedroom where Robby was waiting.

Martha stood in the kitchen motionless for a moment. She reached for the faucet handle and turned it. She cupped her hands together and collected a scoopful of water. She lowered her face and welcomed the sudden sting of the cold against her skin.

ALEX

Your mother wants to take me shopping for school," Alex told Robby when he returned to his bedroom with cookies and Cokes. "Apparently she thinks we need to *bond*."

"I'm sorry," Robby offered from where he was lying on the bed. He had one arm crooked underneath his head. "She's usually not this annoying, I swear."

"I can handle your mother," Alex said with a grin. He leaned over Robby, bent down, and lowered his mouth to Robby's lips. The kiss was soft but fast. Robby turned away before their tongues met.

"Not yet," he said. "I want to, Alex. More than anything. You know that."

Defeated, Alex slid to the bedroom floor and pressed his back against the edge of the bed frame. "What are you so afraid of, Robby?"

"I'm not afraid of anything," he said.

"Bullshit," Alex countered. He reached back and handed Robby a soda. "You're scared to kiss me."

"I've kissed you," Robby said. He cracked the can open and it made a fizzing sound. He slurped at the soda bubbling out of the aluminum mouth.

"But not a serious kiss," Alex reminded him.

"What if we can't stop at one kiss? What if we want things to go further?"

"I'm not gonna lie to you, Robby. I won't fight you off."

Alex could hear the smile in Robby's voice when he said, "I know."

❖

Robby LaMont had taken over Alex's life. For the last month, Alex had found every excuse possible to be by Robby's side. They spent hours listening to every Metric song ever recorded, poring over Alex's collection of comic books, watching classic horror films with the lights out, holding on to each other in the dark, and lying together in silence blocking out the world around them.

Nothing else mattered to Alex, except for Robby. Even Jillian seemed like a distant memory now. And it had been days since Alex had thought about his mother.

Two days after they'd met in the driveway, Alex walked into the pizzeria and quit his job. While Bunny stood by stunned and Sue Ellen lingered around the register, probably hoping for a good-bye kiss, Alex turned and looked at Tommy and said, "See ya around sometime," before walking out the door.

"What gives?" Tommy texted him later that day.

"I met someone else. I hope you understand," Alex texted back.

He hadn't heard from Tommy since.

Alex devoted the next month to discovering all he could about the new guy in his life. Robert Joshua LaMont was a complicated boy with a sensitive soul and a penchant for saying the corniest things. He rarely talked about his life back in Pittsburgh, hardly mentioned his mother and stepfather, and didn't usually speak unless spoken to. He preferred to blend in with the crowd, disappear in a room full of strangers, keep his thoughts and observations to himself.

Physically, the two young men were a sharp contrast to each other. Robby was smaller, softer, and amusingly awkward. He always looked disheveled: baggy shorts hung from his hips, an oversized T-shirt draped his body like a bedsheet, his hair needed to be cut since the start of summer and his bangs half covered his deerlike eyes. He moved as if he were wounded, like someone had hit him one too many times.

Almost like he was permanently damaged.

Yet Robby thrilled Alex. Just one glance at the guy, and Alex felt high. Robby gave him an incredible rush, and he was feeling addicted.

❖

The moment school started, everything changed for them. No longer could they spend the entire day together. They had to settle for text messages between classes, secret looks exchanged across the cafeteria, and long-awaited reunions after school in Alex's bedroom. It was only the second day of the semester and Alex found himself already living for the weekend when their time together would be unlimited.

"I hate being apart from you all day at school," Robby said, as if he were reading Alex's mind. "It sucks."

Alex opened the package of cookies, slid the plastic tray out of the colorful wrapper. "Yeah," he said, "but it would suck a lot worse if people found out about us."

Robby sat up in bed, propping himself up on one arm. "What do you think they'd do to us?" he wondered aloud. "Do you think they'd kill us? Or do you think they'd even care?"

Alex offered Robby a cookie. "I hope we never have to find out," he said.

"I've been hit before," Robby confessed nonchalantly.

Alex tried hard not to let the surprise on his face show. *Why in the hell would somebody hit you?* "By your stepdad?"

"No," he said. "He's harmless. By people at school. Other guys."

Despite the bad taste forming in his mouth, Alex bit into a cookie. "Why'd they hit you?"

Robby lay back down. "Why do you think? Nobody likes a fag. Not even in Pittsburgh."

Alex stood up then. He stayed by the edge of the bed for a moment, just looking down at Robby. Their eyes met and Robby reached up, extending a hand to Alex. "Come be next to me," Robby invited.

Alex slid into the bed and curled up against Robby. He wrapped an arm around the boy's small frame and held him tight. "I won't let anyone ever hurt you again," he promised.

Robby blinked back his tears and said, "I know that." He wiped his cheeks with the back of his hand and added, "That's just one of many reasons why...I've fallen in love with you."

ROBBY

I want you to be careful," his mother said to him. Robby stood, motionless on the bottom step of the staircase. His hand was frozen midair, just an inch or two above the banister. His backpack was heavy. His shoulders ached. He just wanted to go to his room, put on his headphones, lie down, and think about Alex.

Until dinner.

Then he'd be forced to sit at the table, surrounded by the awkward silence floating between his mother and Harley. There would be no sound but silverware tapping against plates. Harley chewing the ice from his glass of sweet tea. His mother occasionally drumming her manicured nails on the tabletop. She was bored. Harley was restless. They were maddening. He tried to skip dinner with them as often as he could. Just to avoid the dim hatred they tried to hide from each other, but that still showed in their eyes.

Robby turned to his mother. She was standing in the living room, bathed in afternoon sunlight pouring in the bay windows. She wiped her hands on a dish towel before placing them on her hips. "You know what I'm talking about," she persisted.

He shook his head. "No...I don't."

"You…and Alex," she continued.

Robby looked away, avoided her eyes. His mother was the last person in the world he wanted to talk to about Alex. She wouldn't understand. Besides, there was no way he could put into words the way he felt about Alex. "What about us, Mom?"

"Are you…" she began, but stopped suddenly. She moved closer, slid her fingers through the spindles in the staircase. "Are you sure this is what you want, Robby?"

Robby waited for a moment, hoping his mother would leave him alone and go back in the kitchen to finish making another one of her tasteless casseroles. When it became clear she wasn't getting the hint, he let out a big sigh. He turned around, slipped his backpack off, and sat down on the third step from the bottom. "Why do you want to talk about this?"

"Because I'm your mother."

He folded his arms across his chest. "It's embarrassing."

"What are you embarrassed about?" He could hear a smile in her voice. "So…you're gay…I get it."

Robby felt a sudden wave of nerves rock his body. "I don't want Harley to find out. He'll make a big deal about it… like in Pittsburgh…when those guys painted those words on our sidewalk."

"Okay, okay. We don't have to tell Harley. In fact, you probably won't see him much tonight. He's decided…not to have dinner with us anymore."

"Good."

"But…I think he already knows."

Robby looked his mother in the eye. "He does?"

She nodded. "Yeah…I'd say so."

Robby felt his body relax, but only a little. "Mom…does everybody know? I mean, do you think people can tell…just by looking at me?"

"Why should that matter?"

"Because…I'm tired of people making fun of me…I'm tired of getting hit."

"Has somebody hit you? Who? Who did this to you?"

"Nobody here," he said, then added, "yet."

"Well, if they do…"

Robby stood up. "But you can't protect me, Mom. No one can." He moved quickly up the stairs. When he reached the top, he turned back and his words drifted down to his mother. "Except for Alex."

JILLIAN

From the moment he entered the room, greeted the class with a delicious smile and a smooth-as-silk "Good afternoon, class. I'm Mr. LaMont," Jillian hung on his every word.

The way his mouth moved when he called her name sent heat spiraling through her body. She raised her arm from where she sat in the front row of the classroom and answered, "Here."

On that first day of class, Harley LaMont became a new hunger for Jillian. By the end of the first week, she was feeding herself on the coy winks he tossed to her, the way his gaze drifted down to between her legs, attempting to catch a peek. She kept her knees together and tried her best to pay attention to his longwinded lecture on Nathaniel Hawthorne's *The Scarlet Letter*.

Yeah, yeah, yeah. I get it. Hester Prynne had an affair with a married man. Big deal. She knew what she wanted.

And Jillian knew, without a doubt, her middle-aged English teacher wanted her in the worst way. He wasn't very tall, was losing his hair, and had a bit of a beer belly, a permanent five o'clock shadow, and big hairy knuckles. But there was something about him that electrified Jillian's body with white-hot desire.

She watched him like a moving target, pacing back and forth, enrapturing her with every gesture he made. She felt heat swim between her legs when he became so intense about Hester Prynne's crime of passion, he broke a piece of chalk in two while writing on the board.

On a Wednesday night, Jillian tore a piece of paper out of her binder, scribbled a sentence on it, and slipped it inside the Chinese wish box that sat like a trophy on her bedroom bookshelf. Her words read: *I want Harley LaMont to realize he can't live without me.*

He smelled like sex. That sweet and spicy combination of soap, aftershave, and sweat was a wild aphrodisiac to her. It made Jillian want to get as close to him as possible to inhale, the need for her touch emitting from his skin. He made her want to touch herself.

Constantly.

She found any excuse she could to go to his desk, lean in, and ask him about a word in Hawthorne's classic novel. All the while, she was imagining licking his neck, biting his skin.

She raised her hand and he came to her and kneeled down beside her desk and she showed him the haiku she'd written titled "Harley."

She asked him, "Is this what you're looking for…Mr. LaMont?"

And he answered in his deep and soft voice, "You're definitely on the right track, Jillian."

JOHN

John was stunned. It showed on his face. Martha stood, framed in the arched entryway leading to his kitchen. He knew she regretted her words, her observation. Her blond hair was down and hung loosely around her beautiful face. She was dressed for her morning run in gray sweats and a black hooded sweatshirt. Her pale green eyes looked tired, stressed, but still shimmered with a deep desire for him. She took a sip of late-morning coffee from the oversized mug in her hand and said, "I'm sorry, John. Did I just say something wrong?"

He was in the living room, standing near the antique coat rack and the old grandfather clock—heirlooms passed down to him by his mother, before the nursing home and the Alzheimer's. Out of the corner of his eye, he saw Siran: her face, her smile, her long, thick ebony hair. He blinked and reminded himself it was just a photograph. She was gone. Long gone. They had buried her a month ago.

Has it already been a month? Jesus, Siran, when you coming home? Me and the kid need you here.

"Wait a second," he said, half to the family photo on the mantel and half to Martha. "You think my son is...*gay?*"

Martha stammered. "I'm sorry...John...it's not my place...I shouldn't have...I thought you..."

"You thought I *knew*?" he asked her, hearing his own voice start to rise. "I don't understand, Martha. Did he come right out and say this to you? Did you catch him doing something? I mean, what the hell happened?"

"John...I think you should talk to Alex. He's your son. I'm just—"

"Just what? Our new neighbor? Come on, Martha, you're more to me and you know it. I took the day off to spend with you...in *private*."

John was worried Martha might start to cry. He could hear it in her voice, the strain to hold back her tears. "I don't know *what* I am to you."

He shook his head, frustrated. "I need you tell me about my son. I don't understand this. I thought him and Jillian—"

She turned away from him and returned to the kitchen. He followed her. "It's not for me to say," she said, facing the window above the sink, the hot September sun streaming through it. The beautiful golden light on her face was like a halo. It made John want to reach for her, hold her, make love to her.

Damn it, Alex. What have you done now?

"Don't leave me in the dark here," he insisted. "We're talking about *Alex*. He's my kid. If he were...a...queer...I think I'd know about it. I mean, I'm his father, for God's sake."

Martha took a step toward him. He noticed her grip on the coffee mug tightened, her knuckles paled. "And I'm Robby's mother. I had to face the truth a long time ago. I can't change the fact he's gay. And I wouldn't want to. This is no one's fault, John. We can't look for someone to blame for this. It is what it is. But we're their *parents*, and we need to be there for them."

Martha exhaled, let out a heavy sigh of sorrow and regret. She put the coffee mug down on the counter and released the handle from her grasp as if she were giving up, letting something go.

In that moment, John saw the truth, the reason she wanted him to know about Alex. Why it was so important for him to really see what she already had. Although he knew he was in love with Martha, John missed his wife more than ever as he stood in the middle of the kitchen. He wanted her there. Siran would've known the right words to say to Alex. She would have held him and reassured him they still loved him, no matter what.

John knew he needed to say the words Martha couldn't. He had to articulate them, give life to them so they would be real. So the truth would finally be out there. He swallowed and his mouth felt dry, his words were cracked. "You mean…are you trying to tell me…Alex and Robby…our *sons*…"

Martha placed a palm against his cheek. He was so overwhelmed by her soft touch, he had to close his eyes and breathe. "They're in love with each other," she said through her fresh tears. John blinked his eyes open as if her words were stinging his sight. He nodded to let her know he understood what she was saying, the important meaning of her words.

Martha leaned into John, mouth first.

John closed his eyes again, and inside, he imagined he was holding on to the round edges of the Earth for dear life.

As if everything he knew and loved depended on that moment.

Right before they kissed, Martha spoke. "Just like we are."

MARTHA

Martha kept looking for any form of kindness she could find in Alex, any sign he was allowing her into his life. There was none. The seventeen-year-old was relentless, stubborn, and his behavior toward her bordered on cruel.

He sat in the backseat of the car, arms folded, eyes turned defiantly out the window, headphones locked into his ears to avoid any form of communication.

Robby sat next to her in the passenger seat. He fidgeted and was anxious. "Are we almost there, Mom?"

"I took a wrong turn but I think we're headed in the right direction now," she explained. "I've never been to Locust Grove before."

Robby sighed, shifted in his seat. She couldn't see his face, but she was almost certain he rolled his eyes. "I don't know why you just don't get a GPS."

She took a breath and fought to regain her composure. This shopping trip was turning out to be much worse than she could have imagined. Ever since Alex had entered their lives, Robby was no longer her best friend, her confidant, her source of eternal positive reinforcement. She used to shine in his eyes. Just a month ago, he acted as if she could do no wrong. Now she was the last person in the world he wanted to spend time with. Every second of Robby's life now revolved around Alex.

"Like Harley would ever let me do that," she said. "You know how old-fashioned he is. He probably doesn't even know what a GPS is."

Robby rested the side of his face against the window. "You're the one who married him."

Martha braked at a red light and the car jerked a little. "Can you give me a break here, Robby?"

He turned to her and she caught a flash of anger in his brown eyes. "God, Mom. What's your deal?"

"My *deal*?" she repeated. "I don't have a *deal*. I'm trying to be nice. I'm trying to do the right thing. But neither one of you will let me."

Robby folded his arms across his chest and balled his fists. His body—the insolent pose and pouty rebellion—mirrored Alex's in the backseat to a T.

"Do you know how *fucking embarrassing* it is to have your mother take you shopping for school?" Robby shot at her. "This was your dumb idea."

"Oh…my…*God*." She was unable to hide her shock or her rapidly approaching breaking point. "Did you just say *fuck*?"

"So what if I did?" he challenged her.

She wanted to slap him. She wanted to pull over into a gas station, drag his ass into a restroom, and shove the first bar of soap she could find into his filthy mouth. Instead, she reached for the air-conditioning control knob and cranked it up. She struggled not to yell. "I'm *trying* to make this work."

Robby's mood and tone softened. Maybe he was scared of her. "What are you talking about?"

She moved her hand in a circular motion, including the

three of them in her midair whirlwind of a gesture. "*This*. You. Alex. I'm trying to understand it."

He pulled away from her then, withdrew as far as physically possible. He looked like he wanted to melt right through the door and land on the hot asphalt of the road. She heard the hurt in his voice, heavy and thick. "What's there to understand?"

She shook her head, hoping the tears she felt rising would go away. The last thing she wanted was for Alex to see her cry. He'd think of her as weak. Maybe he'd even use it against her. Convince his father she was an emotional basket case. That she was bad news.

"Maybe that was the wrong word," she said, the calmness in her voice restored.

"Then what are you saying?" he asked.

She breathed deep before she answered. "The whole situation is complicated."

His body tensed and the coldness crept back into his words. "Only because you and Alex's dad made it that way."

Martha turned onto a road leading them to an overcrowded outlet center, lined with an endless selection of stores. She squeezed the car into an empty parking spot. She killed the engine and looked at her son. "What exactly are you implying, Robby?"

He gave her a smirk, an arrogant little shrug of his thin shoulders. "I'm not *implying* anything," he said. "We all know what you're doing with him."

"What are you talking about?" she asked, her face reddening. "Who knows?"

Alex suddenly leaned forward from the backseat. It was then Martha realized the music he'd been listening to was muted. She had no idea for how long. His words crept into her ear like a vicious tickle, whispered with more hidden meanings than she could count.

"Everybody knows," Alex said.

Martha couldn't take her eyes off the boys. Not because she didn't trust them or she was worried they might behave inappropriately in the clothing store; it was because watching Alex and Robby interact gave Martha the rare opportunity to witness love—*real love*—firsthand.

It wasn't just evident in the way they communicated silently with their eyes, or in the hidden meanings of their inside jokes causing them to dissolve into rings of eye-tearing laughter. She saw it when they looked at each other, as if they needed one other just to breathe. She heard it in the delicate way Alex said Robby's name. *"Robby...come here. I like this shirt. What do you think?"* Robby only beamed and nodded in happy agreement.

Martha hung back and gave them space, trying her best not to have a breakdown in the middle of the store. While she was glad Robby had found someone to love in Alex, she was distraught over the fact her son and his gay lover weren't only suspicious of her affair with John, they were adamant she was having one.

This is a small town, Martha. Don't screw this up. What in the hell are you thinking? His wife just died. People will talk.

And what about Harley?

Martha had just taken an aspirin with a gulp of water from a drinking fountain when Alex emerged from the men's dressing room. He was wearing a white tuxedo shirt, unbuttoned to the middle of his chest, and a pair of black slacks. His feet were bare and his wild black hair was unusually messy.

She offered him a smile. "You look nice—"

He stopped her by raising his hand. He held it up like a crossing guard holding back traffic. "Jillian will be here soon," he said. "She just texted me."

Martha tucked her purse under her arm and squeezed it hard against her body. "Oh?" she said.

The hallway outside of the dressing room was unusually quiet and deserted. Just the drinking fountain and a gift-wrapping counter closed until the day after Thanksgiving, according to a handwritten sign taped to the wall. There was a vending machine at the end of the hall, but not another soul in sight. The silence made Martha uncomfortable, nervous.

"Yes," Alex continued in the same authoritative tone. "She has a car. She'll take us home. You can go now."

Martha shook her head and locked her knees. She was determined to stand her ground.

"I don't understand," she explained. "We came here together. So you could buy some new clothes for school."

"No," he replied. "We came here because you want me to like you so you'll feel less guilty about what you're doing with my father."

"Alex," she said. "That isn't fair. I haven't done anything wrong to you."

His hand went up again. "You're free to leave, Mrs. LaMont. We'll bring Robby home later. He'll be safe with me."

This little prick has bossed me around for the last time.

Wait. No. Remember, Martha. He's angry. His mother just died. He's still a child. "But…your clothes…how will you…"

"Pay for them?" he completed. She nodded, still fighting for control in the conversation. As usual, he was winning the war. *Damn.*

He unbuttoned the rest of the tuxedo shirt he wore. He glanced at the price tag. "I wasn't expecting you to buy my clothes for me, Mrs. LaMont. I brought my own money. In fact, I gave some to Robby so he could go to the snack bar. Didn't you know he was hungry?"

"He should have told me," she said. "I'm his mother."

"Then you must have seen the bruises. The scars."

Martha felt her face pale. "What are you talking about?"

Alex maintained his matter-of-fact tone. "From all the times he got beaten up."

"What?" she said. "Nobody hit my son. I don't know what he told you—"

Alex's expression shifted. He looked at her with pity. "You really had no idea…did you, Mrs. LaMont?"

She struggled with the impulse to reach out to him, to take him into her arms, hold him and let him know everything was okay. Either that or slip her hands around his long neck and squeeze the hate right out of him. "My son had some… problems…at his school in Pittsburgh," she explained, then added, "Alex, I'd really like it if you called me Martha."

He stepped toward her. She backed up and was surprised when her body met the wall. His black eyes narrowed and his bottom lip trembled. She glanced around, eyeing an emergency exit door a few feet away. "Why?" he asked. "Because you're sleeping with my dad?"

She stared Alex directly in the eyes. Martha didn't flinch. "No," she said firmly, refusing to appear intimidated, "because it's my name."

His eyes washed over her, taking inventory of her from

head to toe. He looked disgusted by what he saw. And it reminded her of Harley's expression at the dinner table. Like the sight of her made him sick. "What kind of a person does that?" he demanded. His voice had climbed in volume and bounced off of the wall behind her.

"Excuse me?"

"You're married. You live across the street from us. My mom just died. How can you do it?"

Martha felt dizzy and for a second she feared she might faint. Darkness was trying to creep in from all angles and directions. She felt sweat roll down the center of her back, seep into the waistband of her shorts. "I don't think...you should talk to me that way."

Alex took a step back. He gave her a second going-over. He grinned, finding her ridiculous. "Why?" he said, trying not to laugh at her. "Because you're an adult? I thought grown-ups were supposed to set a good example for us. You've done a real shitty job of that one, *Martha*."

"You don't know anything about me, Alex. You think I'm trying to take your mother's place."

He exploded and his voice ricocheted in the hallway like a round of bullets. "Don't ever talk about my mother!" He slammed his fist into the wall beside her head. Martha lifted her hands, covering her face. Immediately, she started to sob.

"I'm sorry," she told him through her heavy tears. She could barely get the words out. It felt like she was choking on them. "I know it's wrong."

Alex took a huge breath and when he exhaled, his rage seemed to fade away in an instant. "Then *why* are you doing it?" he asked, as if he were her therapist. He sounded twice his age, wise and concerned. "Why can't you just leave my family alone?"

He turned away from her and started to walk away, back into the dressing room. His hand was on the wooden round handle of the accordion door.

Martha wiped her eyes and swallowed her emotions. She stopped him with her words. "Alex," she stated. She decided to play the only card she had left. "If I walk away now...Robby goes with me."

He grinned, shook his head, laughed a little. "You're out of your mind," he said. "Robby isn't going anywhere."

Alex slid the door closed, ending their conversation.

❖

The two women collided outside of the clothing store. Martha was leaving and Jillian was about to make her entrance. Immediately, Martha noticed the teenaged girl was refusing to make eye contact with her. It only took a few moments for Martha to realize why.

"Hello...Mrs. LaMont," the young blonde offered. She was a striking girl. Tall with thin, narrow features. She could have been a ballerina. Or maybe even a runway model. Yet her tough no-nonsense attitude destroyed the beauty in her vulnerability. She was too raw, too crude. Too uncomfortable and angry in her own skin. Maybe she hated the world.

"The boys are inside," Martha explained, "shopping."

They stepped away from the entrance to allow other people to enter. "Yeah," Jillian said. "Alex texted me a while ago."

Martha could see Jillian was nervous. She toyed with the ends of her ponytail, pinching the ends of her hair as if they were shouting out her deepest, darkest secrets and she wanted to silence them.

"Are you his rescue party?" Martha asked.

Jillian gave her a strange look and shifted her weight from

one foot to the other in her pink and white sandals. "I don't... understand what you mean," she said.

Martha sighed. "Jillian, your best friend hates me. You know it. I know it. We both know it."

"I don't think he...*hates* you. Maybe he just doesn't know you. I mean, none of us really do since you're new in Harmonville and stuff."

Martha forced Jillian to meet her stare. "But he's in love with my son."

Jillian nodded, and for a second a glimmer of innocence floated in her eyes, and it moved Martha. "I know," she said. "He's hardly said a word to me in weeks...since you guys moved here."

She's lonely, Martha thought. *She's young and pretty and lonely. And Harley already knows this. He spotted her, approached her—had a conversation with the poor thing at the church bazaar two weeks ago.*

"Tell me," Martha said, with caution, "do you like your classes this year?"

Jillian's eyes widened a little and her breath quickened. "Yes."

It's too late. He's already made a move on her. She'll be the next one.

"Any particular favorites?" she asked.

"No. They're all the same," Jillian answered with a nervous laugh. Martha raised an eyebrow—an expression of disbelief. It seemed like Jillian needed to clarify her answer. "Except English. It's pretty cool. Harley...I mean...Mr. LaMont...he's a good teacher."

Martha wondered what Jillian's home life was like. She was probably the daughter of a single mother. No father around. Long days and lonely nights spent alone. And now her best friend was neglecting her because he was in love.

My God, I bet she has nobody.

Martha knew she had to say something. She had to warn her. Even though the girl was practically a stranger, Martha felt she owed it to her. "Just be careful, Jillian," she offered.

Jillian appeared frozen with fear, or deep concern. Only her mouth moved when she spoke. "About what?"

Martha looked deep into the girl's beautiful, inquisitive eyes. "Everything you learn."

Jillian fumbled a little when reaching into her purse for a tube of lip gloss. She uncapped it and Martha watched as the young girl rolled the shine across her lips. She rubbed them together and grinned as the flavor pleased her. Like it was new to her.

Like tasting the thrill of danger for the very first time.

October/Hoktember

ALEX AND ROBBY

"Do you realize your mother is sleeping with my father?" There was amusement in Alex's voice. He peered through the screened wall of the enclosed back porch and up to the sky, blackening as an autumn storm inched closer. He ran a hand, nervous and quick, through his dark hair, his index finger sticking for a second on a knotted curl.

Robby was nearby, swaying in the back porch swing, his face damp from the humidity. The rope chain of the swing made a high-pitched creak each time Robby moved. The soles of his bare feet were brushing lightly against the cracked wood of the verandah. His arms were folded across his chest and he appeared to be staring out at the woods, behind the house.

"I figured as much," Robby replied, still rocking. Back and forth. Back and forth. "I knew my mother would have an affair. My stepdad ignores her all the time. And when he doesn't, he's kinda mean to her."

The porch light burned and hissed, bathing them in a pale yellow light. Alex continued staring through the dusty screen, standing a few feet in front of Robby and the swing.

Robby spoke again. "I'm sure it won't be long."

Alex felt a knot of nervous anticipation, tickling his lower back. "For what?"

"For my stepdad to find out."

Alex turned and looked at Robby. As usual, he found himself catching his breath. He felt invigorated by their love. He'd felt invincible since he first met Robby. The intensity between them was like a vibrant electric spark, an illumination crawling and slithering its way around, up through the wooden planks of the porch until it touched their feet, their ankles, their legs. It was a feeling of being consumed, eaten alive, and Alex both loathed and loved it. "Wouldn't divorce be easier?"

Robby's mouth lifted into a soft smile and Alex exhaled, feeling his cheeks burn. Robby pushed away strands of brown hair from brown eyes that seemed to hold captive a permanent sense of sorrow. "Nothing is simple for my parents. They like the excitement of it all. They thrive on it. He likes to say horrible things to her. She likes to forgive him. They've been this way since I can remember."

"Well," Alex responded quickly, "at least we're not like that."

The porch swing suddenly came to a halt. "Me and you?" There was a hint of urgency in Robby's voice, as if the anticipation was choking him, too. He coughed a little and his eyes watered. "What do you mean, Alex?"

Alex turned away, back to the woods and the looming black clouds. He shuddered as thunder cracked above him like a broken limb. "If our parents are in love, what does that make us? Your mother is married. My mother killed herself. You and I are—" Alex heard the metal links of the rope chain squeak as Robby stood up. The porch swing banged against the house and more thunder rolled like flung dice over the sky. Robby moved slowly, across the porch, until he stood only inches behind Alex.

"Twisted," Robby finished and his words fell on the back

of Alex's neck, causing him to wince a little from the sensation. "Or incredibly lucky."

Alex closed his eyes as the rain began to fall. Slivers of it cut through the tiny holes in the screen and cooled the heat in Alex's face. "Yeah…I feel lucky," he breathed.

Robby stepped even closer, invited by the hopefulness in Alex's voice.

"Robby," Alex began. "I'm not sure what we are—you and I—but I'm not scared of it."

Robby stood, trembling. He felt the warm October rain cover his hands, his arms. He felt the Southern air wrapping around him tighter and a trickle of sweat shooting down his spine. He stared at the back of Alex's neck, at the warm and inviting Armenian skin. On instinct, Robby raised his hand, wanting to touch Alex, to feel the burn of his skin beneath his thin fingers. His hand, controlled by lust, moved toward the space between Alex's shoulder blades, a place where Robby secretly suspected a person's soul was kept.

The moment became electric. As the tips of Robby's fingers made contact with Alex's black T-shirt, a flash of lightning illuminated the landscape in front of them. In a quick second, the cement patio and the backyard were revealed: the old marble birdbath, the barbecue grill still in desperate need of cleaning, and the cheap patio set with sun-faded cushions.

The bolt of lightning had struck a nearby power line causing white-hot sparks to dance down from the trees and land like fireworks in the overgrown Georgia grass. The porch light was killed by a sudden power outage, and the two boys stood beneath the silver sheen of a summer moon, with Robby's right palm pressed against Alex's soul. Alex's shoulders tightened and he grew tense, but only for a second. As he exhaled, he felt Robby's arms sliding around his waist from behind, and the two of them were embracing. Robby placed his chin on Alex's right shoulder, pressing his body against Alex's spine, and in a gentle whisper breathed the words, "Show me your island."

❖

Alex held Robby's hand tightly as they ran through the maze of trees behind the house. Exhilaration surged through Alex as he led the way. Together, they dodged hanging tree limbs, jumped over broken branches, kicked up clouds of red Georgia mud as they raced across acres of land, welcoming the rain and the metallic moonlight against their skin.

Within seconds, they stood at the edge of the small lake. Only about a mile in circumference, the lake ended to the right and led to a larger lake to the left.

Robby suddenly tightened his grip on Alex's fingers. "I can't swim," he confessed in the dark.

Alex, empowered by the moment and the raw energy ravaging his mind, replied, "Don't worry. I'll help you."

Alex unbuttoned his faded jeans and stepped out of them. He peeled off his wet T-shirt and discarded it like a rag. He stood, peering out to the distant island, in a pair of boxers. He ran a hand through his wet hair and scanned the calm surface of the lake.

Robby, nervous and panic-stricken by his modesty, fumbled with the button on his shorts. Alex immediately sensed his hesitation and offered, "It's okay, Robby. It's only me." Robby slipped his shorts and T-shirt off and stood before Alex in white briefs, as if waiting for some form of approval.

Alex moved toward him, his feet sinking into the red clay. "Never be ashamed of who you are, Robby," he instructed. Without warning, he kissed the side of Robby's face, his lips brushing across Robby's left cheek.

"With you, I feel safe," Robby stammered. "Does that sound stupid, Alex?"

"It's fifty-two yards to the island."

"Is that far? I can't even see it from here."

"I want you to hold on to me and don't let go."

"Okay. But what if I'm too heavy?"

"Are you kidding? I can carry you. Easily." Alex guided both of Robby's arms around his neck and without another word, Alex dove into the water. Robby held his breath as he felt the two of them go under. The sensation sent a stinging pain through his veins. He locked his arms around Alex's neck, but worried Alex might not be able to breathe. He loosened his grip, just a little, as he became aware of his body against Alex's. As Alex moved them through the water, the front of Robby's body rubbed and ground against Alex's skin. Flashes of immense pleasure triggered in both of them. The feeling was so intensely arousing Robby feared he might black out.

He felt Alex guiding them to the surface of the water. They emerged, gulping the sticky October air in unison, catching glimpses of the night's sky. They slid back down, beneath the water, and continued to swim. Their legs moved in synchronization, jetting them through the murky lake. Alex could feel Robby's weight pressing against him. He welcomed the feeling, seduced by it, and didn't fight it or question it.

Alex brought them up for air again. They were only a few feet away from the small island. He could feel Robby's heartbeat pulsing against his spine. Robby coughed a little, his mouth only inches away from Alex's ear. "You carried me the whole way," Robby said, in a half gasp.

"I told you we'd make it," Alex replied.

At the shore of the island, Alex stood up in the shallow water, took Robby's hand, and led him to land. Their feet sank deep into the red mud as Alex showed Robby the way to the oak tree, the only resident of the tiny island. *"Quercus macrocarpa,"* Alex announced, and Robby stared at him blankly. "It's the name of this tree. It's a burr oak. It's been here for years."

"This is the island?"

"My hiding place," Alex confessed.

"It's small."

"It serves its purpose."

"Is this where you came, the day you found your mother in the garage?"

The question caused Alex to pull away from Robby a little. "I don't talk about that day."

"You can talk to *me* about it," Robby assured.

"What's there to say? My mother was very unhappy and she didn't want to live. She hated Georgia. She wanted to go back to Chicago. Her family lives there. They're Armenian," he said, adding, "Like me."

Robby stared at the tree, reaching out and touching the bark with his left hand. "Maybe that's why my mother's in love with your father. He needs her because he's so sad. And because she's always so lonely."

Alex shrugged, trying to distance himself from the memory of discovering his mother's body hanging from a wooden beam in the garage just two months ago. "Maybe," he said. "Let's not talk about this anymore."

"I'm sorry."

"Our parents can do what they want. It has nothing to do with us."

"I hope my parents *do* get divorced. They hate each other." Robby turned back, toward the house, the trees, their lives. "I can't see home from here."

"Exactly," said Alex, sitting down at the base of the tree. "That's why I come here."

Robby sat quickly next to Alex, shivering a little. "I like it here."

Alex's eyes burned with curiosity as he said, "You know what I've always dreamed of? Building a house here. Just a little house, but a place all my own no one can get to."

"That sounds nice, Alex."

"Maybe we should do it."

Robby wasn't sure what Alex was implying, so he said cautiously, "Build a house?"

"Yeah. It would be cool. We can borrow my dad's rowboat and bring the lumber and the tools out."

"I'm not much of a builder."

"Then I'll build it for us."

"For both of us?" Robby's voice cut through the darkness and Alex could hear the pleading in it, the desire to be wanted and accepted and loved.

"That way we can be safe, Robby. We can have a place to come to and no one will ever mess with us. Just you and me. Together."

"A house on our own island. That would be cool. We should do it."

"We can start planning it tomorrow."

Even in the dark and through the rain, Robby could see the excitement flicker in Alex's eyes. He shivered again.

"You cold?"

"A little."

"Sit closer to me." On impulse, Alex wrapped an arm around Robby's thin shoulders. They both fell silent, hushed by the lull of the water, the rain, the drowning of their hidden fears. Robby sat, mesmerized by the rhythm of Alex's breathing, watching his chest rise and fall. He closed his eyes and listened to the sounds around him. It was then that he felt Alex's lips against his. Robby opened his mouth, inviting Alex inside. The kiss was gentle and soft and left them both craving more.

"Are you going to let me love you, Robby?" Alex asked, his words mixing with the rain and falling tenderly onto Robby's lips. "No matter what?"

Robby's eyes fluttered open. Staring deeply into Alex's, he replied, "I already am."

JILLIAN

Jillian came up with a plan to finally get what she wanted.

Harley made it a point to mention three times in class he'd been appointed the chaperone for the Halloween school dance. He said it was his "punishment for being a newbie."

"Do you have a date?" she asked him once they were alone in the classroom, no other student in sight. Outside, in the main corridor of Harmonville High, students shuffled past the door, moving like dazed cattle from class to class. "For the dance?"

He smiled at her and she fought the strong desire to kiss him. "You mean, am I bringing my wife?"

Jillian nodded in reply. For a moment, Martha LaMont's beautiful face flashed in her mind. Her gorgeous blond hair, her perfect smile, those peaceful green eyes. She was one of the nicest people Jillian had ever met.

How can I do this to her? She's never done anything wrong to me. She isn't evil like Sue Ellen Freeman.

Each time Jillian thought of Martha, she felt a huge wave of guilt wash over her. So she did her best to keep Harley's wife as far away from her conscience as possible.

That included never uttering Martha's name aloud.

"She's staying in. Passing out candy," he explained. "Which really means she'll find any excuse she can to go visit the lonely widower across the street."

Jillian shook her head with disapproval. "She should be with you," she decided. "I would be…if I were her."

"Well, you're not her," he said. "And for your sake, that's probably a good thing."

Jillian thought about unbuttoning her blouse, or lifting her skirt to reveal she wasn't wearing any underwear. She contemplated sitting on the edge of his wooden desk, opening her legs and letting him touch her. She glanced down at his thick fingers, the dark hairs on the back of his big knuckles. She felt her body throb for him.

I need to get out of here…before I do something dumb.

Jillian forced herself to regain her composure. She shifted her body, covered her chest with her binder and the assigned paperback copy of Shakespeare's *Measure for Measure*. "I'll be there," she promised.

"Oh yeah?" He cracked another smile, and she couldn't help imagining what his mouth would feel like on her skin. "I'm looking forward to seeing you there."

She stood there for a moment too long, gazing at him. She let her eyes lower, stopping for a second to rest on the front of his khakis, his crotch. For a brief second, she imagined him naked, what it would feel like to have him thrusting against her.

Jillian shook the image away and moved to the door. Her hand was on the knob when she looked back and said over her shoulder, "Look for me…I'll be the one in the red cape."

❖

Jillian was a woman with only one thing on her mind: seduction. She knew she had to look good. And it was going to take a lot more effort than a shower, some shampoo, a little eyeliner and blush.

Luckily, her mother was working a double shift at Applebee's before hightailing it to Griffin to spend the weekend with some trucker she'd met named Jackson. She tried to convince Jillian he was her long-lost soul mate. Jillian predicted her mother would be brokenhearted in a week and would demand Jillian help piece her back together with a carton of ice cream and constant reminders that Delilah Dambro deserved so much better than jerks like Jackson.

Until the next *badass* came along.

Jillian spun her plan into motion early Saturday morning. As soon as the neon orange *Open* sign clicked on in the front window, Jillian rented her adorable (and somewhat slutty) costume from the shop on Jonesboro Road. She popped over to Starbucks for a toffee mocha. She made time for a much-needed mani-pedi at her favorite nail place near Target. She stopped in at Salon La Vie in Stockbridge for some ultra-platinum highlights and a trim.

At home, she tweezed and plucked for an hour, soaked her body in a coconut lime bubble bath, shaved her legs, slathered her skin with tangerine-scented moisturizer, took the time to put on false lashes, concentrated on every detail of her makeup, and smoked a cigarette on the back porch while a fresh October rain started falling.

At seven o'clock, Jillian slipped into the leather and lace corset and the crinoline black tutu. She pulled on her mother's favorite knee-high black boots and slid her arms through the sleeveless red velvet hooded cape. She tugged a pair of elbow-length black satin gloves over her hands before spraying a few blasts of her mother's imposter perfume on the sides of her neck and breathing in the intoxicating smell of desire.

Moments later, Jillian stood in front of the full-length mirror hung on the back of her mother's bedroom door. She smiled at the reflection, impressed she was unable to recognize herself at first glance. She didn't look like a high school student, and she certainly wasn't dressed like a virgin.

Jillian looked hot, and she knew it. There was no way Harley LaMont would be able to resist her.

❖

Before Jillian entered the overdecorated gymnasium, she wasn't sure what reaction her costume would get. She purchased a ticket from Mrs. Potts, her awestruck elderly math teacher, and positioned herself in the open doorway. She was prepared to wait for the response she hoped she'd get—but the anticipation lasted less than a second. The shift in the room was immediate and intense. Heads turned. Mouths dropped open. A few just pointed and stared, enraptured or envious. Jillian giggled on the inside, feeling invincible and victorious.

Finally, they knew who she was.

That she was *alive*.

Jillian took a step inside the gym and nearly slipped on the shiny wooden floor. She steadied herself and continued to move through the crowd of familiar faces at a slow and sultry pace. She was in no hurry. She wanted to bask in every second of their shock and surprise. Dance lights—electric blue and pink and white—pulsed and throbbed over her body in perfect sync with the rhythm of the song blasting out of the DJ's enormous speakers.

At once, Jillian felt their eyes on her, crawling all over

her skin like invisible fingers. She was like a goddess, a movie star—*I'm their motherfucking queen.*

As Jillian walked past them, she saw their blurred faces in her peripheral vision, but she refused to acknowledge their presence. No eye contact. No words. No recognition at all. For as long as she could remember, they'd made Jillian feel invisible. She was just another girl sitting in the back of the classroom.

But not tonight.

Tommy Freeman was there, dressed as a farmer in overalls. His date—a freshman with freckles and braces—was wearing a sequined cowgirl outfit probably once belonging to her country-western singing mother. Jillian heard Tommy say her name—shouting to be heard over the music—but she ignored his voice. "Is Alex with you?" he asked more than once.

Hunter Killinger was lurking around the dance, looking as ridiculous as ever. He was dressed retro-style like it was 1984, complete with a pair of black Ray-Bans. His idiot followers were wearing similar outfits, like refugees from an episode of *Miami Vice.* Hunter licked his lips when he saw her, as if she were a dessert cart being pushed through a restaurant dining room. He was starving and wanted a taste of *everything* she had to offer. Jillian was both repulsed by Hunter's reaction to her—and proud of it. Not once had he ever noticed her, given her the time of day.

Not like she wanted to be lusted after by a pig like Hunter.

"Hey, Little Red Riding Hood," Eric Lowe yelled in her ear, like a perverted air raid. He was Hunter's faithful sidekick—half as popular, half as attractive. "I got something for you to *ride.*" He grabbed his crotch and pointed to it with his skinny fingers—in case she missed it.

Jillian thought of Alex and ached for him in that moment since the DJ was playing "Help I'm Alive" by Metric. He would be so bummed when she called tomorrow to tell him. She wished he was there with her, if only to witness the incredible response she was getting.

By tomorrow morning, I'll be legendary.

And there he was.

Harley LaMont was standing near a card table covered with a punch-stained white tablecloth, a bowl half-full of the sweet-smelling fruity drink, and several stacks of red plastic cups. At the sight of him, Jillian felt the air pause in her lungs. She felt the space between her legs dampen and the beat of her heart triple in speed. He was dressed as Dracula, complete with a long black cape, a high-collared tuxedo shirt, and a red silk bow tie. His dark hair was slicked back and he'd penciled in a widow's peak. His face was ghostly pale, caked with white makeup and powder. His full lips seemed dangerously appealing.

He took one look at Jillian and the word "wow" stumbled out of his mouth.

"Hello, Harley," she purred. As she stood next to him in her thigh-high shiny black boots, Jillian looked him straight in the eyes—he and she were the same height now. In his gaze, she saw hot desire shining back at her. She reached around him, and the inside of her arm—the soft black satin glove—grazed gently across his torso. She lifted the plastic ladle in the punch bowl.

He turned and placed a hand around her wrist. "No," he insisted. "Allow me."

She released the ladle and it slid back into the red liquid, disappearing beneath a layer of floating orange slices. "Damn," he said and she started to laugh.

"No worry," she offered, struggling to be heard over the contagious beat of the hot song. "I wasn't thirsty anyway."

He licked his lips and when he spoke, Jillian could feel his warm breath on her cheeks. "Are you hungry?" he asked, with half a grin.

She glanced at his chest and let her eyes wander down to the front of his black pants. She fought the impulse to reach out and touch him, to grab his cock and squeeze it. She knew he had to be hard. "I'm starving," she answered.

He leaned in and his words crawled into her ear, causing a vibrating shiver to whirl through her body. "Meet me in the auditorium in ten minutes," he instructed.

She smiled back and asked, "Are we going to see a private show?"

He glanced around, nervous and cautious. Worried they'd been speaking too long, that people might start to wonder, speculate, talk?

"No," he said before he walked away, "we're going to create one of our own."

❖

For a moment, Jillian wished someone would've stopped her.

She walked alone down the deathly quiet and eerie main corridor of Harmonville High. It was dark, but strips of moonlight shot through the small windows where the ceiling and the walls met. The bluish silver light cast drifting shadows across the metal faces of the goldenrod lockers. Some of them looked like hands moving toward her, trying to hold her back.

Her boots made an echoing sound with each step she took.

The reverberation of the *tap, tap, tap* seemed haunted and ghostly to her, like a voice from the grave crying out *stop!*

She paused for a moment outside the door to Harley's classroom, where discussions of Hawthorne and Salinger and Shakespeare took place. Where she sat in the front row, swooning like a lovesick idiot day after day. Hoping Harley would see her, pay attention to her, return the same level of deep desire. She wondered if her classmates saw it—how much teacher and student wanted each other. Did they feel the intense heat in their suggestive words and lingering looks? Would they be shocked by what she was about to do? With a married man? The old guy who taught English? *That's disgusting.*

Jillian hoped she'd find Martha LaMont at the end of the long hallway. It didn't matter if she was pissed off or hysterical—or even if she glared at Jillian with heavy disappointment and anger dancing in her green eyes. "Please don't do this," she imagined Martha pleading. "He's my husband. He took a vow."

"I'm so sorry," Jillian said aloud and the sound of her own voice surprised her when it filled the empty space, cutting through the chilly air in the corridor.

Jillian almost turned back when she thought of her mother. *This is exactly what she would do—everyone else be damned as long as I have a good time.* Jillian felt angry with herself for a brief moment. She'd worked so hard to prove to everyone she was *nothing* like her mother. She would never sleep with a guy just because he paid her a compliment. She wouldn't get stuck in some small town in Georgia, waiting on tables. No, Jillian knew she was destined to end up in Manhattan, dressed to kill at cocktail parties, flirting with beautiful rich men, climbing out of taxicabs into the slush and the snow, dining in restaurants her mother never even dreamed about.

Damn you, Delilah Dambro. Why didn't you leave this place when you had the chance?

The vague memory of her father flickered in Jillian's mind—but only for a few seconds. Each time she tried to remember his face, the deep hollow of his voice, the roughness of his hand in hers—it was becoming more and more difficult. She'd only been five when he left.

Never to be heard from again.

No one in town seemed to remember her father—except for Alex's crotchety neighbor, Mrs. Gregory. "He fixed my car once," she shared when pressed for details one afternoon when a twelve-year-old Jillian had cleaned the old woman's house for ten dollars. "But the damn thing broke down a week later."

❖

Jillian was surprised to find the door to the auditorium was unlocked.

Harley must have beaten me here. He's anxious.

She pulled the door open and stepped into the dark theater. She was blind, couldn't even see her hands in front of her face when she held them up. She turned back, afraid, retreating from her planned rendezvous out of fear, second thoughts.

Instinct.

The stage lights clicked, springing to life with a crackle and a wild buzz. Jillian could feel the warmth of their glow from behind her. She turned and there was Harley, standing center stage.

She stood, frozen for a moment by the majestic sight of him. A smile exploded across her face—she couldn't help or hide it. Just one glance at him, and she was delirious. Giddy. Temporarily insane.

"Did you get lost?" he asked with a grin. He lifted up his arm, extending a hand in her direction, waiting for her to meet him onstage.

Jillian walked slowly, taking in the beautiful view. Harley looked strangely out of place, dressed as Dracula and standing on the set of the school's production of *Into the Woods*. He was surrounded by beautiful trees, and Jillian was amazed at how real they looked from the audience. She slid her gloved hand into one of the pockets of her red velvet cape and retrieved her tube of lip gloss. She coated her dry lips with a layer of cherry-flavored shine before starting her rise up to the stage. She climbed the seven wooden steps in the orchestra pit and exhaled an invisible cloud of nervous energy when she reached the top.

Jillian made her entrance onstage, stepping into the golden light, to join her Prince of Darkness in the forest. She accepted his hand and was surprised by the incredible force with which he pulled her into his arms. His lips silenced her before she could speak. She felt his five o'clock shadow scraping her cheeks; his stubble was sharp and rough.

The world felt like it tripped into hyperspeed to Jillian. Everything around her was moving so fast. Harley's hands were all over her body, tearing at her costume, grabbing her breasts and squeezing them hard—like he was angry at them. His mouth was covering her skin. He was devouring her whole.

The next thing she knew, they were behind the set—hidden from the audience's view by the trees. Harley had her down on the ground, pressing so hard against her, Jillian feared she might fall straight through the floor of the stage and plunge into the dark depths of hell. She felt pain between her legs, sharp and tearing, and it caused her eyes to fill with hot tears.

Harley was grunting and sweating on top of her, so she

glanced away, in the opposite direction. It was then she realized the trees in the make-believe forest weren't so real after all. They were only painted cardboard and tissue paper.

They were just an illusion.

November/ Noyember

ALEX

"Tell me something about Armenia," Robby suggested. Alex stayed silent and took another sip from the bottle of Armenian whiskey his mother used to stash behind the washer in the laundry room. He'd been saving it for a special occasion. After the three of them had survived Thanksgiving dinner together with Robby's caffeinated mother, Alex's subdued father, and Jillian's slightly buzzed and recently single mother, Alex felt it was the right night to break out the stolen booze.

"He doesn't like to talk about Armenia," Jillian answered for him.

"Why not?" Robby pushed. "Isn't that where he's from?"

The exasperation was heavy in Jillian's voice. Alex grinned at the sound of it, at her lack of attempt to hide her irritation. "He was born *here*."

Robby's gentle smile didn't falter. Alex admired him for not taking Jillian's bait and engaging in a contest of *who can be the bigger bitch?* "Well, I know *that*," he said with a small laugh. "I guess I'm just curious."

Alex took another sip and passed the whiskey to an all-too-eager Jillian, who tilted back the bottle and gulped the liquor like it was water. She stopped, choked, coughed. "Jesus!" she fumed. "Damn. This shit is strong."

"I warned you," Alex reminded her.

"Can I try some?" Robby asked, apparently not wanting to be outdone by a girl. Jillian shot him a look of "whatever" and handed him the bottle.

Robby took one sniff of the liquid and his eyes watered. He quickly gave the bottle back to Jillian with a dismissive "no, thank you."

Alex stood up. The three of them were sitting in the dark on his island. The only source of light was the reflection of the late November moon floating on the still surface of the lake water.

The three of them had stumbled off the back porch and raced to the water's edge, climbed into a metal rowboat belonging to Alex's dad, and headed out across the lake. Robby and Alex had sliced the water with sturdy oars, sweating and paddling to the shore of the island. Jillian smoked a cigarette, guarded the bottle of whiskey between her legs while threatening them if they splashed her, she'd ruin their lives.

Even though the tension between Robby and Jillian was thick and awkward, Alex was thrilled to be spending the night with two people he loved most in the world. Besides, the bantering and bickering flying back and forth between his boyfriend and his best friend was often amusing. Alex knew the only reason Robby and Jillian were jealous of each other was because of him. They both wanted to be the one thing in the world that mattered most to him.

He leaned up against the sturdy trunk of the oak tree and looked down at the two people sitting at his feet. Robby with his soft skin and shaggy hair, and those big brown eyes Alex could never refuse. Jillian with her low-lying blond ponytail and graceful, long body and the sexy way she pouted when she didn't get her way. Alex suddenly remembered a time when they were little when Jillian insisted she was going to be a dancer. He smiled at the random memory, having forgotten about it over the years.

He looked at Robby and said, "Apricots."

Robby looked up at him and asked "What?"

Alex felt the sudden need to be closer to him. He sat down behind Robby on the cold, damp ground, resting his cheek on the boy's shoulder. "Apricots come from Armenia," he said. "They're the best in the world. Ask anyone."

"It's true," Jillian chimed in. "Except in Armenia, they're called *dziran*."

Alex took the bottle from her. "How'd you know that?"

"How do you *think*?" she tossed back at him. "Your mother taught me. She used to make that dish...what was it called?"

Alex took a sip of the whiskey and answered, "*Missov dziran*," before adding, "It's disgusting."

Jillian shot him a look. "I liked it. She used to send me home with leftovers."

"Yeah," Alex said, avoiding the sadness shifting into Jillian's gaze. "I remember." He wrapped his arms around Robby and closed his eyes.

Jillian jumped to her feet. "If you two start making out, I'm stealing the boat and leaving you here."

Alex smiled and could feel Robby shudder with laughter.

"Are we allowed to smoke on this island?" Jillian asked, digging into the pockets of her sweatshirt. "Or is there a no-smoking policy in this lovely place?"

Alex tightened his grip on Robby. "We're free here," he replied. "We can do whatever we want."

❖

It was well after midnight when Alex received the text. The message was short, simple: *Can you meet me?*

It was from Tommy Freeman. Concern spread through Alex like a house fire, yanking him out of his buzz and sobering him up instantly.

Alex texted back, without hesitation: *Where?*

He looked out his bedroom window and across the street. The lights were off at the LaMonts'. Alex contemplated texting Robby to see if he was still awake, to tell him he was going out to meet Tommy. It seemed like the right thing to do.

No, Alex decided. *Let him sleep.*

A half hour later, Alex was on foot and shivering, approaching the empty parking lot of the pizzeria. He found Tommy sitting on a cement parking block beneath the pale yellow glow of a fluorescent street lamp, nursing a forty-ounce bottle of Old English. The pizzeria was dark and deserted. Chairs were stacked on tables. The neon open sign was turned off. Outside, there wasn't a soul in sight.

Except for Tommy.

"Was your Thanksgiving that bad?" Alex asked the football player.

Tommy looked up. His eyes were swollen and bloodshot. He was either really drunk or else he'd been crying. "I didn't think you'd come," he said, sounding wounded.

"I figured it was important." Alex sat down next to Tommy on the cement block beneath a posted blue and white handicapped parking sign. He winced a little when the cold concrete stung his skin, right through his thin black jeans. "And you're my friend."

"Am I?" Tommy asked. "You haven't said shit to me since that kid moved to Harmonville."

"Robby," Alex said. He felt guilty saying Robby's name, like he had no business being in the pizzeria parking lot with

Tommy in the middle of the night. But Alex was certain nothing intimate would ever happen again between him and Tommy. All of that was in their past.

Besides, Alex thought, *I'm not in love with Tommy. I never was. My heart belongs to Robby.*

Tommy drained the bottle before asking, "I guess you're *with* him, right?"

Alex nodded. The temperature had dropped since he was on the island with Robby and Jillian earlier. He could see his breath each time he exhaled. "Yeah, but don't tell anybody. I don't want trouble for him."

Tommy turned the empty bottle on its side and kicked it gently with his foot. It rolled away from them, across the broken asphalt, disappearing into the dark. "No one would believe you're a fag, Alex. They all think you're sleeping with Jillian."

"Keep it that way," Alex said. "Hunter and the other guys—I don't want them messing with Robby."

Tommy's voice broke then. He tried to fight tears off, but they cut right through his words. "Why'd you come?"

"Why'd you ask me to?"

Tommy wiped his eyes with the back of his hand. "Guess I just needed someone to talk to."

"About what?" Alex asked. "Your old man on you again about stuff?"

Tommy nodded and sniffed. "Yeah, you could say that. He told me after dinner I was the biggest disappointment in his life."

Alex gave Tommy a soft, playful punch in the arm, trying to lighten the mood. And to stop thinking about his mother, what her body looked like hanging from the rope in the garage. Her face. "Man," he said, "don't listen to him. Tommy, your dad's an asshole. Everybody knows it."

Tommy turned to Alex and his tears were visible then, glistening on his skin beneath the pale light above them. "You're right," he said. "He *is* an asshole. But…I kinda think he's right about me. I *am* a big disappointment."

Alex shook his head and held Tommy's gaze. "Don't talk like that."

Another tear spilled down his cheek before he said to Alex, "I didn't get a scholarship."

Alex felt his mouth go dry. Stunned, all he could say was, "What?"

"Most of the recruiters—they all thought I was no good. I might have to stay here, Alex. In Harmonville."

"That's crazy," Alex said, dismissing the seriousness of the situation with a small, nervous laugh. "Nobody knows football better than you."

Tommy started to sob then, as if his heart were breaking open wide and every emotion he'd kept hidden was pouring out into the parking lot at once. "My dad can't even look at me now," he whimpered. "He hates me, Alex."

Alex put a comforting arm around his friend's shoulders. It felt so strange to hold Tommy again, to touch him.

I want to go home. To my mother. I need her right now.

"You're going to be okay," Alex said, to both of them.

Tommy shook his head, struggling to reel his feelings back in. "Can you imagine what he'd do…if he knew…about me…how I like guys."

Alex pulled away from him. "You're gay, Tommy. You can say it. So am I. It's not a big deal."

Tommy turned and stared into the darkness in the distance, beyond the edges of the circle of the lamplight. "Yes," he said to the night around them. "It is."

December/Dektemper

JOHN

Martha decided to stay in the car at the cemetery. She told John if he needed her, she'd be right there waiting for him. He knew her words were true. Martha was a good woman, which made him feel like it was okay to fall in love with her so soon after Siran was gone.

Alex also stayed behind, sullen and stubborn in the backseat with his headphones on, refusing to show one ounce of emotion to anyone. He was still doing his best to ignore Martha whenever she was around. In the few instances Alex did say something to her, it was to remind her of her place—of the love and regard he deeply held for his mother, and the blatant lack of respect he had for her.

John figured he was on his own that Christmas morning—his son and the woman he loved would stay in the warmth of the car, leave him to suffer through his sadness alone. So it surprised him when he heard one of the car doors open—that annoying electronic beeping sound. He was kneeling in the grass next to Siran's headstone, placing a beautiful bouquet of flowers down, when he sensed his son standing behind him. John stood and faced the seventeen-year-old.

"Alex?"

"I didn't think you missed her anymore," his son told him, staring him directly in the eye.

John slipped his hands into the side pockets of his gray pea coat and shivered. "Of course I miss her. Every single moment of every single day."

"Why?" Alex challenged. "You have Martha now."

John nodded. "I know," he said. "And it doesn't make any sense to me, either."

Alex glanced down at the headstone, the flowers. "I know you're going to marry Martha."

John looked over Alex's shoulder, to the car. To Martha's face in the passenger window. He knew she was worried, concerned. "That's not possible, Alex."

Alex grinned a little, lifted his eyes up to the December sky as if he wanted to laugh at God. "Anything is possible," he declared.

"Martha is married to—"

"To my boyfriend's stepfather. I know. I think about that all the time, Dad. It creeps me out."

John flinched at the word *boyfriend*. Even though he knew what Martha had told him about Alex and Robby was true, it still punched him in the gut to hear his own son admit it. As much as he loved Alex, it was so hard for him to understand it. *How could someone be gay?*

"You said something to me a few days after your mom died," he said. "We were on the front porch. You said something in Armenian."

Alex folded his arms across his chest and clenched his fists. *"Haskanum em,"* he answered. "It means—"

"It means *I understand,*" John said. "That's exactly what your mother would want."

"For me to understand you're sleeping with the lady who lives across the street?"

John shook his head. "If she were here, she might help me understand *you*. Whatever this thing is you have with Robby—"

"Well, she's *not* here!" Alex shouted. "And maybe if one of *us* would've *understood* how lonely and sad and homesick she was, she'd still fucking be here!"

John reached for Alex, but his son jerked back with a staunch warning of "Don't touch me."

"What do you want me to do, Alex? You want me to spend the rest of my life alone? Feeling guilty over your mother? Is that what you want? Huh?"

"I want you to miss her as much I do!"

"That's impossible, because I miss her *more*."

"Bullshit. All you care about is Martha. The two of you make me sick."

"I haven't said one word about what you're doing with Robby. I stayed out of it."

"Don't do me any favors, Dad. I'm gay. I'm in love with Robby. Deal with it!"

"And I loved your mother very much. But I also love Martha. She makes me happy, Alex. Why is that so hard for you to understand?"

Alex's composure collapsed then. He crumbled right in front of his father. Thick tears sprang from Alex's eyes and burned his cheeks. "Because," he stammered. "I never even got to say good-bye to her."

John grabbed his son's arms, trying to hold him up by his elbows, but Alex slid right out of his grasp. He fell to his knees, then to the ground. He was on his side, pressing his body against the earth above his mother's grave, as if he wanted the world to split open wide and swallow him alive.

John turned toward the car, afraid and unsure. But Martha was already there, running across the cemetery, rushing past

John, and dropping to the ground to reach Alex. She pulled the boy into her arms, holding him close, soothing him with her soft voice and touch while he sobbed uncontrollably for his dead mother.

Martha fought back her own tears. In that moment, John realized how strong she was inside. "Don't worry," she whispered to Alex. "It's going to be okay."

John swallowed the lump of sadness clenching the sides of his throat. A sense of peace crept over him as he stood, watching Martha comfort his son. In John's heart, he knew Martha was right. That somehow, everything really would be okay.

JILLIAN

Jillian had just slipped another piece of paper inside the Chinese wish box when her mother appeared in the bedroom doorway, wide-eyed and fire-faced. "What in the hell is *this*?" she demanded.

Jillian glanced down to the yellow piece of paper in her mother's hand. Test results.

"What the fuck?" Jillian yelled. "Did you go through my purse?"

"I was looking for a lighter."

"Why? I don't smoke."

Delilah's voice cracked the air around them. "Don't lie!" she shouted, waving the paper violently, as it were about to burn her. "Is this true?"

"What do you think?" Jillian spat back. She moved away from her mother and stood facing the window. She looked out at the front lawn, across the street to the beautiful Christmas lights strung around the neighbor's house. "Like mother, like daughter...isn't that what they say?"

Delilah stepped into the room. Jillian could feel her mother's words pounding against her back. "You better do something about this, Jillian. Or, what...you wanna end up like me? Is that it?"

Jillian reached out and placed her palm against the cold glass. She closed her eyes. For a moment, she saw Alex in her mind. She drifted for a second, deep into the memory. He was younger. Ten. Maybe eleven. He was waiting for her in his navy blue ski parka and red mittens. "Wanna go play?" he was asking her, just like he had a million times. She would nod in agreement and follow him around the neighborhood. They would laugh and chase each other. They would build things with their hands. They would lie on the grass and look up at the stars and the moon. They dreamed aloud about places they would go when they grew up. Together. Just the two of them.

Jillian opened her eyes. She hated the fact their childhood was long gone. She knew, no matter what, they would never get those moments back. Their lives were too complicated now. Never again would they have time to run and play.

"I'd rather die than get stuck here," Jillian answered her mother.

MARTHA

Jillian," she said. "What are you doing here?"

The young girl was standing on the LaMonts' front lawn, shivering in the moonlight.

She'd found Jillian by chance. Martha was across the street, ready for the clock to strike midnight to celebrate the new year with John, Robby, and Alex. She suddenly remembered the jumbo bag of frozen pizza rolls she'd purchased last week and stored in the freezer in her garage.

"I'll be right back!" she hollered over the music and frivolity. All three men were sitting around the kitchen table playing a highly competitive game of Yahtzee.

"Bring us something to eat, Mom!" Robby yelled back.

"I'm on it!" she explained.

Halfway across the street, she spotted Jillian. Her back was to Martha, but she was certain it was her. She was wearing a peach-colored blouse and a white denim skirt—hardly appropriate clothes for such a cold December night. Her sneakers were wet and caked with dirt as if she'd been walking through the damp night for hours.

When Jillian didn't answer her, Martha moved around the girl to get a glimpse of her face. That's when she saw the tears streaming down her red cheeks. Her teeth were chattering and she was shaking, almost uncontrollably.

Jillian's tearful gaze was locked on the house, and Martha couldn't decide if Jillian was crushed with sadness or rage. But there was an intense glow in her brown eyes that chilled Martha to the core.

Immediately, Martha slipped off her yellow cardigan and wrapped it around Jillian's thin shoulders. "What's the matter?" she asked. "Honey, we weren't expecting you. Alex didn't tell me you were coming by. He said you haven't been feeling well."

Still, there was no response. Just more tears.

"Of course you're welcome to join us. But you need to calm down first and tell me what's wrong."

Jillian nodded as if to acknowledge Martha's kind words had broken through her semi-catatonic state. That there was hope.

"You want me to go get Alex? He'll be happy to see you. And Robby, too."

The young girl shook her head. "No," she said. "I didn't come here to see Alex."

Martha followed Jillian's line of sight up to the second-floor window, to Harley's home office. His desk lamp was on, filling the window with a soft orange burst of light. But the curtains were drawn, so only Harley's silhouette was visible from where they stood on the lawn.

And then she knew exactly why Jillian was there.

"Who'd you come here to see?" she asked cautiously.

Jillian turned to Martha and answered. "You."

Martha felt her pulse quicken and a cold sweat break out in the small of her back. A terrible wave of nausea swept over her and she covered her hand with her mouth, afraid she might be sick on the dead lawn.

"I don't have anyone else to talk to," Jillian explained. "Mrs. LaMont...I didn't know where else to go."

"Just tell me," Martha begged. Her face was numb from the temperature, from the icy situation unfolding on her front lawn. "I already know what you're going to say, Jillian."

Jillian strangely looked relieved by Martha's words. Her dry, cracked lips lifted into a half-smile. "You do?"

Martha nodded, swallowed, then spoke. "You're not the first."

Jillian wiped at her eyes with trembling fingers. "I didn't think so."

Martha reached for the girl, put her hands on her shoulders, rubbed her palms against her to give her more warmth. "He's done this before," she said.

"Is that why you moved here?" Jillian asked. "Is that why you left Pittsburgh and came to Harmonville?"

Martha looked away, back over her shoulder, to the house across the street. "Yes," she answered.

"How could you stay with him, then?" Jillian wanted to know.

Martha closed her eyes for a moment, remembering the day years ago when she stepped off the train in Pittsburgh, with her ballet slippers tucked inside her purse. There had been so much hope in her heart. She hadn't felt it since.

I was so young then.

"Harley LaMont has broken a lot of hearts," she said to Jillian and to the young girl she once was, still standing in the middle of the crowded train station. "I'm guessing he's ended your affair. And I'm sure he's hurt you real bad."

Jillian stepped back from Martha, rejecting her touch and her words. "You're wrong," she said. The conviction in her voice startled Martha. "Harley didn't break up with *me*."

Martha felt her face begin to crumble. She couldn't be strong anymore. It was over. She was done with this ridiculous charade. Jillian continued, "I ended things with *him*, only he isn't taking it so well."

Martha felt her bottom lip tremble as she struggled to get the question out. She already feared the answer before she asked, "And why's that?"

Jillian pulled the yellow sweater tighter around her small frame and answered, "Because…Mrs. LaMont…I'm pregnant. I'm having Harley's baby."

❖

Martha had already packed two suitcases and placed them in the foyer with her favorite purse by the time he emerged from his office, sauntered down the stairs, and headed toward the kitchen. But her voice stopped him in the pitch-black darkness, speaking from where she sat at the head of the table in the formal dining room. She heard Harley make a slight gasping sound, as if she'd scared him, taken him by surprise.

"Is it yours?" she wanted to know. It was a fight to keep her voice so calm, her tone so nonthreatening.

She heard his palm grazing the wall, brushing over the wallpaper in search of the light switch. He found it and flipped it, illuminating both of them in the middle of their end. It was then he saw the suitcases neatly lined up by the front door.

"Martha?" he said to the luggage, and not to her.

"Is it yours?" she repeated.

He turned and looked at her. For a moment, her left eye twitched as she battled with the overwhelming impulse to pick up the crystal centerpiece in the middle of the table and heave the empty fruit bowl at him. "Jillian Dambro says she's having your child," Martha revealed, her voice quaking under the tight control she was using to prevent herself from detonating in the dining room. "Is that true?"

He didn't answer. No response. No immediate denial. No blaming someone else. Just *nothing*.

Martha pushed herself away from the edge of the table, sliding her chair with such tremendous force the back of it slammed into the wall behind her and gouged the plaster. She rose to her feet with her fists clenched at her sides. The explosion of her voice filled the entire room like a sonic roar, rattling the chandelier above them. *"Is it yours?"*

Harley didn't look at her. He simply nodded, lowered his head in shame, and walked out of the room. She heard him on the stairs, climbing them slowly. Seconds later, the door to his home office closed with a high-pitched creak. Then the opera music started. It filled the second story of their house, and the agony of the dramatic piece—the devastation in the trilling voice of the diva—crashed inside an empty place in Martha's heart.

She walked to the front door. She reached for her purse, slipped the strap over her shoulder. She slid her fingers through the firm handles of her two suitcases, tilting them back on their wheels, and stepping out into the wintry night.

Martha stopped for a moment, in the middle of the street. A half hour ago, just seconds after Jillian left, Martha realized she had choices. She reviewed them again while standing in the road. She could turn back—just like she did twice before in Pittsburgh—and go back inside the house that would never be her home and find a way to forgive Harley.

Or she could continue to the other side of the street, where a man who thought he loved her would be waiting for her— but who really wanted his dead wife to come home. No matter how hard she tried, Martha could never be her.

So Martha chose another alternative: she'd made a call in the kitchen before confronting Harley. And, as promised by the stranger she'd spoken to on the phone ten minutes ago, the yellow taxi pulled up beside her, right on time.

The young driver put her suitcases into the trunk and helped her into the backseat of the cab. Even from where she sat, she could hear their voices, happy and shouting, as John, Robby, and Alex started their ten-second countdown to the new year. Without her.

She waited until they were out of the neighborhood before she leaned forward and asked the baby-faced driver, "What time is it?"

He met her eyes in the rearview mirror and answered, "It's twelve oh five." He smiled at her and added, "Happy new year."

Martha leaned back in the cab. She reached for her purse, opened it, and dug out her wallet. She double-checked, making certain she had enough cash for a one-way bus ticket to Florida.

Part Two

May/Mayis

Robby

Robby never even knew what hit him. He had his headphones on. There was enough time between fourth and fifth period to listen to "Silence Is Golden" by Garbage, a song he'd recently discovered and had been listening to religiously.

Because of the music in his ears, Robby had no idea when or who threw the first punch—what direction the first blow came from. He only felt the pain. It rippled through his body, unfurling in violent shock waves, rushing to every nerve ending.

After the first hit, more came. It was a sudden burst, a flurry, a torrential downpour. A dark storm cloud had been ripped open wide and was sending a thousand pounding fists against Robby's skin.

He could smell them, his attackers. They reeked of dirt, sweat, repugnant anger. They were guys—just like him—but stronger, bigger, vicious. He reached for them with his soft hands, hoping if they knew how gentle he was they'd love him instead of hate him. He made contact with the sleeves of their shirts, the skin on their arms. But no matter how hard he tried to touch them, they kept slipping out of his grasp.

They wouldn't stop. They wanted Robby destroyed.

Dead.

But Robby fought off the blackness. He refused to let the dark win. Instead, he concentrated on the words to the song— even though the music had stopped, had been ripped away from him—he kept playing it in his mind. He sang it in his own muted voice.

When they grew tired of pummeling him with their hard fists, they forced him to the ground, held him down against his will. He stopped struggling when he tasted the bitterness of the asphalt, when he felt the sharp ridges of black bits of gravel pressing into his face.

They used their feet then. The tips of their basketball shoes and cowboy boots collided with his body. The air was crushed out of him, but he kept clinging to every lyric, every line of the song. He refused to let go of it. It was all he had, but it was all he needed.

Then he saw her, and she was so beautiful Robby felt a surge of love explode like fireworks in his soul. She was the lead singer of the band, the goddess with the urgent voice. He smiled at the sight of her, stunned by the halo of golden light bathing her. She was only in his mind, but Shirley Manson seemed real enough for Robby to reach for.

Instead, she reached for him.

She held out her hands and Robby accepted them in his. She pulled him gently into her arms, holding on to him, soothing and comforting him.

She took over the song for him then, singing the words and letting them fall like warm drops of rain into his ears. With each note, her emotions intensified. Robby could sense the moment she began to cry. He knew the tears she shed weren't only for him, but for someone else. Maybe someone she'd lost. Someone she loved as much as he loved Alex.

He could feel the heat of her skin, the incredible amount

of strength and the unbreakable will she was infusing him with. He refused to let go of her. He knew she would never leave him, not until it was all over.

When the kicking stopped, they used objects made of wood. Something broke across Robby's body, splintering into pieces.

In his mind, Shirley tightened her loving grip on his body, cradling Robby against her, and he knew.

How badly she wanted to protect him, shield him with her own skin.

ALEX

"Take good care of him," the school nurse said. Alex couldn't remember her name, but he knew Jillian had christened her the Gila Monster back in ninth grade. Alex silently cursed his best friend because the nickname now seemed really appropriate. So much so that he found it difficult not to laugh at her.

The nurse was a robust woman, squeezed into a wrinkled white uniform, scuffed white shoes. Her hair was a mass of torched red curls. Her face was sprinkled with freckles—flecks of toasted cheese floating on her pink skin. She sat in an armless office chair she used to wheel herself around the tiny room, moving as recklessly as a drunk driver. The chair wheezed beneath her girth and the black wheels skidded across the dingy floor as she came barreling toward Alex. A second before she lost control of the chair and slammed him into a wall, she caught herself by using the palm of her right hand as a brake and gripping the edge of a waist-high yellow counter.

"Jesus," Alex muttered at the sight of the commotion she created.

The nurse was a slob. Her work space was in a state of irreparable disarray: students' personal information spewed out of the sides of overstuffed manila folders, a half-eaten Milky Way candy bar poked out from beneath piles of smudged paperwork. Unopened boxes of tongue depressors and latex gloves covered any empty counter space they could find.

"Do you understand what I'm saying?" she asked too sweetly, perhaps unsure if Alex spoke English since his skin was a few shades darker than hers.

Alex knew the situation was a serious one, but he was distracted by the run in the nurse's opaque stockings. It started behind her left knee, stretching down to the back of her thick ankle. Her flesh, tarnished by purple-blue varicose veins, seeped through the tear in the taut nylon. Alex continued to stare at the run. It was like a scar, a second layer of skin gutted open to reveal a person hidden beneath a Gila Monster's disguise.

Heloderma suspectum, Alex thought to himself proudly. He was still fascinated by the scientific names of things, considering it a personal victory when he knew what they were. He contemplated saying the words aloud, as he was certain the Gila Monster in white would have no idea in the world of science she was better known as *Heloderma suspectum*.

The nurse cleared her congested throat and Alex raised his dark eyes to meet hers. "Are you listening to me?" she pressed.

Alex's voice cracked a little. His mouth was so dry from the lack of air in the suffocating office. The windowless room was no larger than a closet and it reeked of mildew. Alex nodded in agreement and said, "I think he needs an ambulance... ma'am."

The nurse shook her head. "He doesn't want one. He refuses." She reached for a clear plastic jar of cotton balls, sitting on a wobbly black metal shelf bolted into the wall above the messy counter. "I offered to call his mother."

"She isn't home," Alex explained. "She hasn't been home in five months." He thought about making a remark about the affair Martha had with his father, but he fought the impulse.

The nurse continued, as if she were reading a list of her responsibilities and checking them off. "I offered to get a teacher or the principal."

"They're all useless," Alex countered.

"I offered to drive him to the hospital myself." She reached for a brown bottle of hydrogen peroxide and unscrewed the white cap. "The only person he wanted me to find was you."

Alex glanced out of the open door of the office and into the hallway. Robby, half slumped over and half-conscious, sat in an orange plastic and chrome chair much too small even for his skinny frame. As if he sensed Alex's eyes, Robby struggled to raise his head and look up. The right side of his face was beaten and bruised. His eye was swollen shut. His lips were busted and cracked, parched with slashes of broken skin and caked blood. His nose was now crooked and darkening by the second. He searched for Alex, his eyes wandering around the room, fighting to focus. "Well, I'm here now," Alex said, mostly to Robby.

The nurse lowered her voice, wheeled her chair closer to Alex. She picked up the phone. "I'll notify the police."

Alex's jaw tightened. "What for?"

"Robby should press charges against the boys who did this to him," the nurse insisted.

Alex looked down at the adult, stared her directly in the eyes. "You and I both know what this is about."

The nurse didn't falter. "I've heard things," she admitted. "I thought it was just talk."

"Talk?" Alex repeated.

"He's...a sensitive boy." When Alex's eyes demanded a further explanation, she added, "He's...soft."

Alex shook his head, displeased with her description of Robby. "He isn't a *pillow*."

The nurse raised an eyebrow. "Then who is he to you?" she challenged.

Alex felt a strange mixture of emotions clench the sides of his throat. It was a violent feeling, a combination of rage and sorrow. "The boy sitting in that chair is the only person in this entire world who means anything to me."

"It's none of my business," she said, with a dismissive wave of her hand.

The wick of anger had been ignited in Alex. It was a fury he hadn't felt since his mother had hanged herself in the garage last August. "This place is barbaric," he assessed. "A disgusting zoo full of dumb fucks who can't even spell their names right."

"I understand you're upset." She was placating him with her sticky voice again, and it made Alex even angrier.

"The cops won't do dick about this, and you and I both know it."

She was adamant. "No," she insisted, still sounding rehearsed. "A crime was committed."

"It's bullshit. They'll turn the other cheek because Robby is a freak to them. He's a *fag* and everybody knows it."

Her cheeks burned. "Will you lower your voice, please? He can hear you."

Alex had to smile, amused by the absurdity of it all. "Even the teachers talk about him."

She looked away. *Guilty.* "I've never heard—"

"The teachers are more ignorant than the white-trash rednecks they try to tame long enough to teach them the alphabet."

The nurse pushed her chair back, nearly smacking into the wall behind her. "I think I should call someone."

"Who?" Alex waited for her to answer. "There *is* no one to call except me. That's what he told you."

"Maybe you should take him home now." She took a quick, short breath and added, "After the situation with his stepfather, I'm sure the students will be...disturbed by what's happened to Robby."

"This has *nothing* to do with what Mr. LaMont did."

Her emotions started to surface when she said, with a strain, "I know that."

Alex lowered himself so he was eye level with the nurse. He leaned in close and said in his best imitation of a Southern drawl, "Robby's only saving grace in this situation is he wasn't born black."

The nurse didn't even blink, holding Alex's stare. "That isn't fair."

Alex shot words right back at her. "They would've killed him if he were."

"It isn't like that here...anymore. Georgia is a very diverse place to live."

Alex almost laughed. "For who? My mother was Armenian. Look what happened to her."

"It's a small town," the nurse offered, apologizing on behalf of every citizen of Tanglewood County.

Alex forced a tight smile, shoving the ripening wrath into an empty slot in his soul. "No matter how hard you try to understand the life of boys like Robby, you can't. You're a dumb-shit school nurse who doesn't have a clue. Don't sit here in your squeaky chair and try to convince me you understand how we feel or what we go through. Until you get your fat ass up and walk a million miles in our shoes, spare me the sympathy. You're doing a job, counting down the days until you can retire and stuff your face on an overbooked cruise ship." Alex pulled away from her, stood up. He felt revived; surged with pride.

Instantly, the Gila Monster exploded into tears, her cool façade crumbled into delicate pieces. She covered her mouth with her hand, choking on heavy sobs. Her upper body trembled as she leaned slightly forward and cried. Thick, hot tears slid down her face and splashed onto her uniform, into her lap, onto the backs of her freckled hands.

Alex shoved his own hands into the back pockets of his faded jeans. He rocked back on his heels, his big toes stretching and pressing against the inside tips of his worn-thin black and white Converse shoes. "Good God, what are you crying for?" Alex asked, louder than he intended. "You don't need to cry."

"I'm so sorry," the nurse whimpered.

"Hey," Alex offered, his words a feeble apology. "I didn't mean it. It's not your fault, all right?"

"But it *is* my fault," she wailed. "You don't understand." She reached a hand up and grabbed a fistful of Alex's baggy gray T-shirt. "I'm sorry your mother killed herself, Alex. I'm sorry I didn't know anything about you. I found your student file this afternoon and I'm ashamed to say…I've never read it." She loosened the hold she had on his shirt and Alex began to breathe again. "I didn't even know you were Armenian until today. God forgive me, but I just thought you had a nice tan."

"This isn't about me," he replied coolly.

"It terrifies me, what they did to him." Her voice was a hoarse whisper, her words shaky. "I've never seen something like this. Not in twenty-two years."

"Good," Alex told her, stepping back. "The minute this sort of thing becomes routine, we've lost hope."

Slowly, the nurse stood up. She tried desperately to smooth out the wrinkles on the front of her uniform. She tugged at the material around her hips, trying to lower the hemline on her skirt, to cover the front of her knees. She inhaled deeply and then said to Alex, "I'm just like you."

Alex shot her a look, not sure of what she meant. "You don't look Armenian to me."

The nurse wiped at her eyes with her fingertips. She laughed a little, small and nervous. "That's not what I meant, Alex. I live with another woman. We've been together for six years."

Alex was impressed the school nurse had confessed she was a lesbian, but he didn't show her an ounce of approval. "I don't care what you are," he responded. "I just want to make sure Robby and I live until Thursday. As soon as we graduate—"

"It doesn't scare you? The fact he needs you so much. You're both only *eighteen*."

"And in a year, we'll be nineteen. Not much will change for us between now and then."

"How can you be so sure? You're just a child. Both of you are so young. I mean, is this what the two of you really want?" The nurse suddenly reminded Alex of the hostess of a daytime talk show. Her questions felt scripted again, planned.

Alex reached for the bottle of peroxide. He scooped up a handful of cotton balls. "It's not about making a choice. Robby and I found each other. We just knew…"

"For whatever it's worth—"

"I think you and I have said enough to each other," Alex decided. "You're just doing your job."

She lowered her head, her eyes. "Not very well, I'm afraid."

"At least you're here." Alex offered her a small smile. "Do you mind if I clean him up a little? I'd like to get him out of here before sixth period ends. You know what Fridays are like around here."

The nurse straightened the collar on her uniform. "I think Robby would prefer it."

"Alex Bainbridge, you're the only son of a bitch I know who can make the school nurse cry."

Both Alex and the nurse turned toward the scarlet voice in the doorway.

"Have you no mercy?" Jillian Dambro asked. Almost nineteen years old and seven months pregnant, Jillian commanded the room. She was carrying a straw handbag emblazoned with an embroidered pink magnolia on it. She looked at Alex with new sparkling green eyes and waited for an answer.

"She and I were having a private conversation," he explained.

"I hope one of you had the decency to call the cops." Jillian's powerful presence made her appear even taller than she was. Her head turned, sharply, toward Alex. "Stop staring at me like that. We're in the middle of a crisis."

"You're wearing colored contacts," he said, with thick disgust. "I got used to the whole black hair thing, but this is ridiculous."

"I wanted to call the police," the Gila Monster offered. She suddenly appeared nervous, anxious, as if she wanted to be acknowledged. Alex had figured it out long ago—Jillian had that type of effect on people. Everyone she met suddenly wanted to become her best friend, her disciple.

The nurse turned to Alex and came to Jillian's defense with, "I think she looks like Bettie Page."

"Thank you, Giselle," Jillian replied to her and the nurse beamed, her thin lips curling into a tortured smile.

"Green?" Alex continued. "Your eyes are *brown*, Jillian."

"Alex, can you try to focus on the issue at hand, please?" she responded. "I paid eighty bucks for these things to make myself feel better about resembling a bloated sea creature. Will somebody please tell me what happened to Robby, or do neither one of you give a shit?"

Alex let out a sharp breath. "Can you try to not talk like a call girl for one afternoon?"

"Don't get pissy with me. I got my fat ass down here because Mrs. Gregory told me a bunch of fuck wads tried to bash Robby's skull in."

In the hallway, Robby shifted uncomfortably in the tiny chair he'd been forced to sit in while the others around him argued over his welfare. Alex knew how much it bothered Robby to have people make a fuss over him; he hated to be the cause of someone's anxiety. Alex stepped forward, knowing he needed to lighten the mood. He threw his words at Jillian. "You look like a giant watermelon." It worked. Robby tried to smile and his shoulders relaxed a little.

Jillian glanced down at the white maternity shirt she was wearing, which was sprinkled with tiny pink and green polka dots. "Oh my God, I do." She turned her back to Giselle and Alex, directed her loud words to Robby. "Sweetie, don't feel so bad. With my new pair of eyes, I look like a fucking slice of fruit."

"Hey." Alex tugged on the short sleeve of her shirt. "How in the hell do you know the nurse's real name?"

Jillian moved, facing Alex again. "She used to write notes for me so I could skip P.E."

"Jillian and I go way back," Giselle gushed.

"Did Giselle tell you that she and Miss Hoffman have been having a hot and heavy affair since we were in the seventh grade?" Jillian asked matter-of-factly. Giselle's cheeks singed with heat, showing her embarrassment.

"Your P.E. teacher?" Alex asked.

Jillian rolled her eyes, tucked a strand of her jet-black hair behind her ear, and shot at him, "Don't be such a cliché, asshole. Miss Hoffman teaches German."

Alex threw a look over at Giselle. "*Ew*. You're doing my old German teacher?"

Giselle moved toward the door, anxious to get out into the hallway with Robby.

"I hate the contacts," Alex told his friend.

"Good," she replied. "Then I got my money's worth." She took a breath and then said, "Jesus, Alex, what in the hell happened today? He looks awful."

"Help me get him out of here," he responded quietly. Jillian nodded in agreement.

In the hallway, Giselle leaned down toward Robby, her mouth only inches from his ear. "It's going to be okay," Alex heard her say. "I know these people love you."

JILLIAN

Jillian had an intense craving for potato chips. She licked her lips as she wedged herself behind the steering wheel of her old Geo Prizm. The car was filled with the faint smell of coconut, thanks to a sun-faded air freshener hanging from the rearview mirror.

"You're so pregnant, I'm surprised you can fit in the car," Alex mused. He sat next to her, struggling to roll down the stubborn window on the passenger side. Robby was silent in the backseat.

"I need to make a stop," Jillian announced as they pulled out of the student parking lot. The hula dancer doll in the back window started to shimmy, shaking her hips provocatively.

"Doritos?" Alex asked.

Jillian shook her head, brushed thick strands of ink-black hair from her newly green eyes. "Pringles," she replied. "Salt and vinegar."

Alex scrunched up his nose. "Those things are disgusting. Don't breathe on me after you eat them."

Jillian clicked on her signal, braked, and made a left turn onto a two-lane highway. "I hate the sight of this town," she said, eyeing a billboard advertising a new housing development. "Every acre, every inch."

"Feeling hormonal today?" Alex opened the glove compartment and started to sort through Jillian's slim CD collection: Metric, Civil Twilight, Yeah Yeah Yeahs, Shiny Toy Guns, Morningwood, the Dollyrots, and Tegan and Sara.

Jillian glanced in the rearview mirror, checking on Robby. He had a strange look in his eyes, as if he were somewhere else, disconnected from the present. Maybe he was imagining the three of them sitting on the shore of Alex's island. He was watching the passing countryside with an expression of soft sadness. The sight of him made Jillian want to cry.

She turned to Alex, who was still looking for the right song to fit the mood. "I have to be to work soon. A five-hour shift," she told him. "I switched schedules with Amber, so I'm off at nine."

"Won't be long before they make you Employee of the Month."

Jillian felt the edges of her eyes start to burn with hot tears. "God, kill me first."

Alex pressed the issue in his usual smart-ass manner. "That's no way for an expectant mother to talk. Where's your hope? Where's your *faith*?"

"Up your ass with the rest of this God-awful place. Don't make fun of me, Alex. I'm serious. I'm pissed off already."

"About what?

"I'm pregnant, *hello*?" Jillian wanted a cigarette. She hadn't smoked in five months, since that fateful December afternoon at the Tanglewood County Department of Health.

"You're eight weeks pregnant. You're going to be a mother," the female doctor with bad breath had said with a strange smile. Her eyes had narrowed like a rat when she asked, "Do you know who the father is?"

In the parking lot, Jillian had smoked her last cigarette, thrown the rest of the pack out the car window as she sped away, furious. Since then, she'd been cursed by terrible nicotine fits.

Alex opened a CD case and pulled out the disc. "Don't bitch at me. *I'm* not the father."

Jillian's gaze darted up to the rearview window again. There was no reaction from Robby to what Alex said. He remained mute and motionless, his gaze locked on the trees they zoomed by. She lowered her voice. "Can we not talk about that right now?"

Alex shrugged. "He already knows. Everybody does."

Jillian felt her left temple throb. "Still, we don't have to bring it up. He's been through enough today."

"And you think talking about his stepdad will push him over the edge?"

"Hey, I ended the situation."

Alex looked down at Jillian's belly, straining against the bottom arch of the steering wheel. "It looks like your timing was a bit off."

Jillian glanced down at the three cigarette burns on the panel of her door. They were in the shape of a triangle. They were history—each charred hole in the gray fabric had a story behind it. Jillian silently ached to be holding her favorite pink lighter—to bring the flame to the end of a cigarette and inhale deeply. She lashed out at Alex. "I don't need this shit from you today, all right?"

"Fine. Sorry."

"And I don't want to listen to music right now!"

"Bite my head off."

Without saying another word, Jillian pulled over to the side of the road. The front wheels of the white car slid onto the grass, wet from the humid air. The car hadn't even fully stopped when Jillian turned to Alex in a rage. "This is bullshit!"

"Why are you yelling at me?"

"Because you're an asshole." On impulse, she opened the car door and got out.

Alex quickly followed, tossing the CD and its case back into the car.

Jillian stumbled around the car, away from the steaming highway. She was a fast-moving blur of white, pink and green polka dots, and faded denim jeans. She leaned against the hood on the passenger side. "Will you get back in the car, please?" Alex asked. "I'm sorry, Jilli."

She folded her arms across her chest, indignant. "Don't tell that to me, tell it to Robby."

"What are you talking about?"

"Does it even matter to you?" Alex stared at her blankly. "Of course it doesn't. That's just how you are, Alex. You never want to deal with the sensitive stuff."

"What are you accusing me of, exactly?"

Tears filled Jillian's eyes and she could tell they took Alex by surprise. In the twelve years of their friendship, Jillian had rarely let him see her cry. She looked away from him. Her voice shook and the edges of her mouth trembled. "You need to be there for him."

"I am."

"No, you're *not*." Jillian started to cry harder and it made her angrier. "He's all busted up and sad inside. Fuck, it breaks my heart just to look at him."

Alex turned back toward the car. "Then don't."

Jillian grabbed the back of Alex's T-shirt, snapping him back toward her. "Why are you trying to ignore this?"

Alex twisted around and faced Jillian. A dark curl dipped down in front of his left eye, and even though she was mad at him, Jillian instinctively brushed it out of his view. "What choice do I have? You want me to go find the guys who did this and put a bullet through their heads?"

"I want you to *care*."

"I know what this is about."

"I told you—"

"Bullshit. You're pissed off because you can't smoke."

"Fuck you."

"And you're upset about working at Value Mart."

"I'm gonna burn the motherfucking place to the ground, Alex!"

He took a breath before he said, "You're scared you're gonna get stuck here."

The words cracked her tough exterior even more. "Are you my shrink now? God, lay off. It's too insane for me."

"The fact Robby got beaten up or because you're pregnant?"

"I'm fucking scared, all right? I know you're gonna leave."

"What are you talking about?"

"Don't try to look all innocent. I know you want out of here."

Alex almost laughed. "I do?"

"After graduation next week."

Alex shook his head. "You're wrong, Jilli. I hadn't even thought about leaving."

Jillian turned to him. Her hair whipped across her face and she tucked it behind her ear with a quick finger. "Well, why not?" she asked. "It's not like there's anything here for us."

"You've thought about leaving Harmonville?"

Jillian wiped at her eyes. "Every day of my life. Since I was twelve."

As was his habit when the topic of conversation became too personal, Alex changed the subject. "It bothers you? My reaction to what happened to Robby today?"

Jillian glanced away, toward the highway, the passing cars and diesel trucks. She nodded.

"Why?" Alex prompted.

"It doesn't seem right," Jillian decided, her Georgian roots clinging subtly to the edges of her cadence, her emotions. "It doesn't freak you out that a couple of redneck assholes decided to use a Louisville Slugger on Robby's face."

Alex and Jillian stood only inches from each other, draped in silence. Their bodies were frozen like victims of a botched game of tag. Jillian felt the hum and vibration of the car, close to her right leg. Alex was leaning against the frame, his left hip pressed against the white metal. They stared at each other, realizing something had to be done. Something they'd often dreamt about, but never dared to speak.

It was at that moment Robby poked his head out of the window in the backseat and proudly declared, "It wasn't a baseball bat. It was a hockey stick." Robby looked to Jillian first and attempted to smile at her. His effort made her tears return. His head shifted to the right and he looked deep into Alex's eyes when he said, "But the stupid thing broke after the first hit."

❖

As soon as Alex got the idea, the world around them seemed to shift. Everything felt as if it were moving faster, sped up to the point where all motion appeared like euphoric blurs of light and sound, bolts and hot splashes of color and noise. The excitement in Alex's voice was contagious, and within seconds, Jillian caught the same disease.

They were still in the car; the three of them were en route to Jillian's house. She was supposed to change her clothes before heading off to Value Mart.

Jillian was nervous, fidgeting behind the steering wheel, still missing the time in her life when she could smoke a pack a day.

Alex was staring at the cover of Hole's *Nobody's Daughter* CD. Her best friend appeared lost in deep thought.

Alex looked up and stared through the windshield at the long stretch of road in front of the car. Jillian felt the sudden rush of energy emitting from his skin like a sudden spark. She glanced at him and he looked like he'd just reached a final decision. It gave her goose bumps.

"We *are* leaving," he announced.

The car swerved a little into the other lane before Jillian straightened it out. "What did you just say?"

Only moments had passed since she'd pulled the car over to the side of the road and waited until Alex had convinced her he would never allow her to suffer alone in Harmonville.

"You son of a bitch," she hissed at him. "I thought you just said you'd never leave me in this place."

"I'm not," he promised. "You're going with us."

"I am?"

"Together," he breathed.

Robby

Robby was in the backseat, flinching and wincing each time the car encountered a pothole or Jillian took a turn too sharply. The pain was searing in his rib cage. He wondered how Harley would feel when he saw the damage done to him. Then again, Harley hadn't paid much attention to him once his wife had disappeared. He agreed to let Robby move in with John and Alex without a fight.

Robby wondered if and when he'd hear from his mother again. There hadn't been a word from her since the postcard came from Satellite Beach, Florida, postmarked on Valentine's Day. Maybe she was mailing him a piece of her heart, from the center of her new life. "I love you," the postcard read. "I'm sorry."

Robby started to smile, realizing he knew Alex better than Jillian did. Jillian freaked out, instantly assuming she was going to be left behind like a big, pregnant dust cloud. But Robby knew Alex meant the three of them would be leaving together.

"No matter what," Jillian once told Robby one night on Alex's island, after she'd finished off a couple of Coronas. "Alex and I will *always* be best friends. We've known each other for twelve years. He's like my twin brother."

In the backseat, Robby secretly gloated over his victory. Despite the fact he'd met Alex only nine months ago, it was obvious he was able to anticipate Alex's words and thoughts better than Jillian. To prove Robby's muted point, Alex said, "The *three* of us. We're leaving."

Jillian didn't hesitate. She didn't protest or question Alex's possibly rash decision. She simply said, "When?"

"Give me a few hours," he instructed.

"What do I have to do?" she responded.

❖

It was like they were planning a bank robbery, a strategic heist that would change their lives forever. They were comrades, spies, quickly rattling off ideas and details. They were gamblers, addicted to the same twirling slot machine that was certain to pay out. Escaping appeared to be second nature to them.

Robby watched and listened from the backseat. The idea became visible, glowing and growing larger by the second, like an overinflated balloon or a pumped-up bicycle tire. It was circling in the air around them, hovering like a two-engine plane sputtering and coughing but sustaining life in the air.

It felt electric.

Alex was clearly in charge, the conductor of their symphony. "We go to your house. Pack your things."

"I only need one bag."

"What about the baby?" he threw back at her.

"I've got two more months to think about her," she countered.

Robby's excitement started to swim.

"We're leaving *tonight*, Jillian."

"Let's do it." She was fearless—the quality Robby liked most about her. Maybe the only one.

"Do you have any money?" Alex asked her.

She nodded. "A hundred and fifty bucks or so in the bank. A check for sixty dollars from my grandma at home. I'm supposed to use it to buy a maternity dress for graduation."

Alex ripped open his backpack for school, tore a sheet of paper out of a notebook. He opened the glove compartment, fished for a pen or pencil. "I've got seven hundred and some change saved up," he confided. "I could sell my comic book collection."

"No." Jillian shook her head adamantly. "No, you can't do that. I won't let you. Those are *way* too important to you."

"I've got three hundred and forty-three dollars and a jelly jar full of quarters," Robby offered, anxious to be included in the plan.

Alex started adding up the figures on paper. "I think we're good," he decided for everyone.

"Good for what?" Jillian asked, struggling to keep her eyes on the road. She was distracted by her own giddiness.

"For us to start over."

Jillian could barely breathe. Robby feared she might go into labor two months ahead of schedule. "Together? The three of us?"

Alex checked his math. "We've got enough money for gas...an apartment."

Jillian and Robby spoke at the same time. "An apartment?" they echoed.

"We're moving in together?" Jillian asked.

Robby was already decorating their new kitchen in his mind.

"If you want to," Alex teased.

Jillian let out a squeal, a celebratory shout. Then, "Fuck *yes*, I want to!"

"We'll go to your house first," Alex explained. "We'll get your stuff packed up and in the car. I'll drop you off at work."

"I'm not going to work," Jillian protested.

"Yes, you are. You need to get your last paycheck," he reminded her.

Jillian nodded, accepting the command. "I'll see what I can do."

"Robby and I will go to my house, grab a few things. Get some clothes."

"Then you'll come get me?" Jillian could barely contain herself. It was evident to Robby she was ready to fill up the gas tank and hit the road.

"We'll be there to pick you up before sundown. I promise."

Jillian breathed deep, caressed her belly with the palm of her right hand. "I can't wait, Alex. This is why I love you. This is why you're my best friend. I would never be able to pull off something as crazy as this on my own."

From the backseat came Robby's voice: "We should've done this sooner."

"This is so perfect," Jillian continued, manic and high. "It's the ultimate *fuck you* to this place. Promise me we'll be out of the God-awful state of Georgia by midnight."

"Shit," Alex said. "If we leave tonight, we'll miss graduation."

Both Alex and Jillian started laughing. Hers was heavy and thick, his was melodic and kind. Jillian shook her head, pushed a handful of dyed black hair away from her fake green eyes, and proclaimed, "It's a ridiculous ceremony for boneheads. We're through with finals. Who gives a shit? I say, the sooner we leave the better. They can mail me my fucking diploma."

"I agree," Robby said, leaning forward and placing a hand on Alex's left shoulder.

"Money might be tight, once we get there," Alex told them, trying to sound practical by giving them a gentle warning—a small dash of reality to mix in with their wild dreams of ultimate freedom.

Jillian clearly wouldn't be stopped. "I don't care if I have to live on rice and water for six months, let's *go*."

Robby winced a little as the pain in his ribs intensified. "Hey, we've been through worse, right?" he offered. His words, his positive energy, his eternal optimism sealed their unified desire to flee their own lives.

"My thoughts exactly," Alex said. "Even if we have to swim to get there."

"I just hope we don't drown first," Jillian said.

Alex gave her a look. "I won't let you," he said. "You know that."

Jillian laughed a little and then said, "This might sound like a dumb question, but where are we swimming to?"

Alex turned to his best friend and said, with deep hope in his voice, "Chicago."

JILLIAN

Once they arrived at her house, Jillian stole one of her mother's suitcases out of the garage and packed her belongings in less than fifteen minutes. The three of them scrambled around her bedroom, ripping clothes from hangers and piling photographs, paperbacks, pairs of shoes onto the growing heap. Once her hair dryer and makeup bag were tossed onto the pile, Jillian climbed on top of her bed, sat down on the overstuffed suitcase, and instructed Alex to zip the thing shut. They struggled and fought with it, but finally won.

She moved across the room to the bookshelf and grabbed the Chinese wish box. On impulse, she turned to her best friend, and placed it in his palm.

She was trusting him to guard her secret desires for her. Until she needed them back.

"I'm ready," she announced, breathless.

❖

After a quick trip through the drive-thru of Dairy Queen, they were back on the road heading toward Value Mart.

"They have two Value Marts in Stockbridge, one in McDonough, and one in Griffin. Why in the hell did we need one in Harmonville?" Jillian wondered aloud, trying to drive and eat at the same time.

"I still can't believe you work there," Alex teased.

"Are you jealous? Because I ended up with a glamorous career?" she replied. "I'll see if I can hook you up with a position there. Maybe if you're lucky, Sue Ellen Freeman will let you feel her up in the break room. The nasty little cow lets everyone else have a crack at her."

"Don't bother," he told her. "We're getting out of this place."

"Amen," she agreed with a holler. "Chicago, here we come!"

"Robby, are you okay?" Alex asked.

Robby leaned forward in the backseat, holding his strawberry milkshake in his right hand. "I've never been to Chicago before. I'm excited."

"It's going to be awesome," Jillian enthused. "Can you imagine? God, Alex, I've always wanted to live in a big city. I can get a really cool job and find a really good school for my daughter to go to. We're finally going to be *living*."

"Chicago was a very special place to my mother," Alex explained. "She loved it even more than Alaverdi." He looked away, out the window, to the clouds above. "In fact, she never really cared much for Armenia." His words were soft and under his breath, spoken in Armenian, but Jillian knew the meaning of them: *"Im mairuh."*

My mother.

"Son of a bitch!" Jillian yelled.

Alex seemed more annoyed than concerned. "What? What's the matter?"

"One of my contacts just fell out." Alex started to laugh. Jillian shoved a paper cup in his face. "Here. Look for it."

"In your ice cream? You're out of your mind."

"Alex Bainbridge, start looking *now*. I'm not going to work looking like a mutant with two different-colored eyes."

For the first time since Jillian had seen him that day, Robby LaMont let out a genuine laugh. The sound of it caused Alex to smile. It was the first indication Robby would pull through the ordeal he'd suffered—and Jillian was grateful for the sign. Soon, everything would be back to normal.

Whatever normal means.

"I don't know why you wasted your money on these stupid things," Alex said to Jillian. "They don't look real."

"If I wasn't driving, I'd kick your ass right now," she threatened.

"Listen, I'm running away with you. Isn't that enough?"

She exhaled as her mood shifted back to euphoria. "My God, you're so good to me, Alex. You're my saving grace. You know that, right?"

ALEX AND ROBBY

Robby felt his breath sharpen in his lungs. It reminded him of the second grade when a female classmate with crooked blond pigtails stabbed him in the left shoulder with a pencil. To this day, there was still a small piece of lead stuck inside him: a tiny black dot could be seen just below the surface of his pale skin.

Robby felt his throat tighten and his mind start to panic, as if he were going to suffocate, hyperventilate. The sensation only lasted for a few seconds. He wasn't sure if it was because his ribs felt cracked or because Alex was touching him. Robby closed his eyes, exhaled. He concentrated on the tips of Alex's fingers as they moved slowly across the top of his hand, trailing across his bruised knuckles like a cool breeze. Robby shuddered a little, opened his eyes, and looked out the passenger window as the car rattled through the rural outskirts of Harmonville.

"I really am sorry," Alex said, now that they were alone. He braked, stopped the car at a lonely red light. The Geo Prizm was packed and they were on their way to Value Mart to rescue Jillian.

Robby glanced at the green numbers illuminated on the

dashboard clock. They were right on schedule, just as Alex planned. The sun was just starting to set.

"You're scared to look at me," Robby said, expecting Alex to pull his hand away. Instead, Alex wove his fingers through Robby's and gently squeezed.

"They hurt you real bad." Alex shoved down the tears rising inside him. Silently, he swore in Armenian and ached again for his dead mother. "I wish I would have been there for you."

Robby tried to smile, but his swollen mouth barely moved. "Then we both would've been in bad shape."

"I can still take you to a doctor—the hospital."

Robby's words were unusually sharp. "No." He pulled his hand away from Alex's. "You said we were leaving. I want to go."

"We are. We are." Alex reached for him again, his right hand drifting up to the left side of Robby's face. Robby flinched a little when Alex touched him, but he welcomed the comfort it offered. The left side of his face had been spared from the beating, but the right side was a brutal confusion of puffy and raw purple, yellow, and blackened skin. There was a thick gash across the bridge of his nose. The white of his right eye was speckled with bits of blood. His lips were cracked and split, bloated so his mouth couldn't fully close. Alex noticed the back of Robby's left hand was scraped, as if he'd tried to fight his attackers off. The words stumbled out of Alex's mouth. "I love you."

Robby turned to him, managing a smile. The sight of his wounds created a deep hollowness inside Alex. He felt like he'd been gutted alive. "I love you, too," Robby replied, his words a soft whisper.

"I hate them for what they've done to you," Alex said. "To us."

"It's a good plan," Robby said, changing the subject. "To leave and go to Chicago. I've never really cared for Georgia. It's never felt like home to me. But Pittsburgh didn't either."

The light turned green and the car lurched forward. Alex refused to switch topics, determined to stay on track. "I never wanted you to get hurt."

"I'm not hurt," Robby responded. "I feel numb." It wasn't the truth, but Robby knew it was what Alex wanted to hear. Pleasing people was a habit for Robby. Being well-liked was not important to him—he didn't like those around him to feel uncomfortable.

"You've just gotten the hell beaten out of you," Alex replied. "I know you're in pain."

Tears sprang to Robby's eyes, surprising him. "I think there were three of them," he stammered.

Alex made a left turn. His knuckles turned white as he tightened his grip on the steering wheel. "Robby, you don't have to talk about this," he whispered, sorry to have brought it up again, for having pushed.

The words spilled out of Robby in a hot stream. "I was leaving drama class, the auditorium. I took the stage door exit to the parking lot."

Alex felt the back of his neck throb with sweat. Guilt flooded over him, burned his cheeks. He was supposed to have met Robby—but was scared he was going to be late for his next class, so he hadn't.

"They were waiting for me. Eric and Hunter…and Tommy. I think it was them. At least that's what the nurse told me while I was waiting for you. Do you think they'll get expelled?"

"It was *them*?" Alex's left cheek nervously twitched a little at the mention of Tommy's name. *What a hypocrite*, Alex thought.

"All three of them," Robby continued. "They called me a fag. Said I should die. But…I didn't."

"What did you do? Did you run?"

"Not at first. But when I did…they caught me."

"What happened then?"

"They told me to suck their dicks."

"And? What did you say?"

Robby turned to Alex, his wave of emotion subsiding. "What do you think I said to them?"

"I hope you told them all to go fuck themselves."

Robby shook his head. "I told them they weren't my type." Alex grinned, and the sight of his perfectly carved dimples eased the pain Robby was feeling in his ribs. "I told them you were the only man who was ever allowed to touch me."

JILLIAN

Jillian had never been polite. It wasn't that she went out of her way to be rude—she simply chose to speak her mind. She'd inherited the trait from her grandmother.

"Are you on a break?" Sue Ellen Freeman asked in her drippy voice, cutting through Jillian's solitude.

Jillian looked up from where she sat on the floor in the middle of an aisle in Value Mart. There was a half-eaten can of Pringles in her lap. Jillian licked her fingertips, sucking the salt and vinegar flavor from her skin. Sue Ellen stood above her, like an overgrown road block in a red, white, and blue smock, black leggings, and ugly shoes. Her permanently damaged hair was a gnarled mess of blond frizz and frosted curls. "None of your business, sweetheart," Jillian replied with a wink.

Sue Ellen's chubby cheeks flushed. She took an uncertain step back. "I was just asking." She stopped, and a strange look crept over her face, as if she'd just smelled something gross. "Oh my Lord, what happened to you? Your eyes. They look strange. They're two different colors..." Jillian shot her a warning look, but Sue Ellen had to keep going. "Were you born that way? I never noticed before."

"You know what?" Jillian continued. "You're the nosiest woman I've ever met in my life. I mean, *really*...don't you have anything else better to do?"

Sue Ellen huffed, folded her arms across her massive chest. "Your shift isn't over yet, *missy*. You're supposed to be on register twelve."

"And where are *you* supposed to be?"

Sue Ellen gestured to the two rows of gardening tools and accessories spilling off the shelves of the aisle they shared. "I'm stocking lawn and garden," she said with a sniff. Jillian contemplated smacking Sue Ellen over the head with a ceramic garden gnome or whipping her to death with a hose—both were satisfying thoughts.

"That seems fitting for a girl like you." Jillian gingerly reached two fingers into the cardboard tube of chips and pulled out three. "I'm sure you have a lot in common with fertilizer."

"Have you lost your mind?" Sue Ellen's thick Southern drawl made Jillian cringe. "You're sitting here on the floor, eating some Pringles like you own the damn place."

"I wish I did," Jillian snapped. "The first thing I'd do is fire your fat ass. You always sound like you have snot up your nose when you talk. Go get a Kleenex."

Sue Ellen straightened her red, white, and blue name tag and said, "I hear you're leaving. You quit."

Jillian swiped at some crumbs resting on the top of her pregnant belly. "Aw, are you sad to see me go?"

"I can't say I am." Sue Ellen smiled, smug. "Running away in shame, are you? A home for pregnant girls without a husband?"

If the words affected Jillian, she didn't let it show. "I'm too young to get married." She followed that up with, "What's your excuse?"

Sue Ellen sighed, feeling superior. "For your information, I'm engaged."

"For your sake, I hope he owns a restaurant." Jillian laughed, amused. "An all-you-can-eat buffet. Otherwise, you might wither away to normal."

The anger flashed in Sue Ellen's eyes and her forehead turned a shade of purple. "If I weren't a Christian woman—"

"Yeah, Sue Ellen, you're a real good Christian. Snaking twenties out of your register every chance you get and giving blow jobs to George in automotive. I'm sure when the neighbors come by your house to say hello, you crawl out from underneath the porch and bark at 'em."

Jillian had pushed Sue Ellen Freeman past her breaking point. "You nasty little bitch." She stepped forward and her scuffed high heels scraped across the dingy floor.

"What are you gonna do, hit a pregnant woman?" Jillian popped another potato chip into her mouth.

Sue Ellen recoiled. "I feel sorry for you. Only eighteen. Knocked up by your psycho teacher. You're filthy trash, Jillian Dambro. So is your mother."

Jillian laughed again and said, "Sticks and stones, *fat girl*. Sticks and stones."

Sue Ellen lost all composure and suddenly shrieked, "What have I ever done to you?"

Jillian rubbed two fingers together, ridding them of salt and crumbs. "Well, back when you were skinny—about four thousand years ago—you were a complete bitch to me in high school. I was a freshman. You were an oversexed senior."

Sue Ellen breathed deep, trying to regain control of the situation. "That was a long time ago. I've found the Lord since then."

"Well, were you hiding from him? You're kind of hard to miss." Jillian swallowed, craving a Wild Cherry Pepsi. "You came up to me in the hallway one day and told me not to worry.

You said I wouldn't look like a boy for the rest of my life. You thought it was funny to embarrass me in front of your slutty friends."

Sue Ellen did a poor job of feigning innocence. "I did no such thing."

"You also told half the county I boned down on your ugly cousin in Riverdale. Like I'd even touch that piece of trailer trash. He's almost as nasty as your brother."

"I'll have you know Tommy just found out this morning he's going to college next year on a football scholarship. They paid for everything for him."

Jillian tried to hold back her laughter. "Well, that's a good thing, Sue Ellen, because Tommy is dumber than a box of rocks."

"Is that why you wouldn't go out with him? Because you think you're better than us?"

"Despite my obvious state of pregnancy, I've never cared for the boys in this town."

"Because you were too busy playing Barbies with your Middle Eastern homo. You're no better than a terrorist, Jillian."

"He's Armenian, you dumb cow. Take a geography class, will you?"

"I don't care if his mother did *die*, he's still going to burn in hell." Sue Ellen's face looked sunburned, she was so mad. "And so will you for having the bastard child of a married man. He was your *teacher*, Jillian. For your information, it's all over the news. I saw it this morning. They even showed his picture so everyone knows what a horrible man he is."

Jillian felt weak. "What are you talking about?"

"One of those news stations did a big story about it. He's a predator. They even said so."

"It was just the local news, right?" Jillian asked. Her mouth felt dry.

Sue Ellen grinned and said with pleasure, "It's *national* news."

"Fuck," Jillian said. "Did they mention my name?"

"No," Sue Ellen said, disappointed. "Lucky for you they didn't interview me. I would've told them the disgusting truth about you."

"It doesn't matter, because everybody knows you're the one who gave Hunter Killinger a case of crabs."

Sue Ellen's nasal whine shot up again. "Are *you* the one who started that rumor?"

Jillian batted her eyes and replied in an exaggerated drawl, "Heavens no. I'm a good Christian. I'm just a simple girl from a small town in Georgia who dreams about marrying a bowlegged truck driver." Jillian laughed again. "Get the fuck away from me. Let me enjoy my last few minutes in this redneck rodeo in peace."

Sue Ellen took another daring step forward. "I hope your baby is born retarded," she spat out. She turned quickly and made her escape, shuffling down the aisle.

"Go with God, Sue Ellen!" Jillian yelled after her. "Stupid bitch."

Jillian took her time finishing the rest of her potato chips. When those were gone, she lifted the can to her mouth, tilted it up, and showered her tongue with crumbs. She chewed like a maniac, angry and anxious. She cursed the day Sue Ellen Freeman was born. She fumed with rage over Harley LaMont and the ridiculous affair she'd had with him. She prayed Alex and Robby were on their way so the three of them could get on the road to Chicago.

Jillian looked down at the dirty floor, smudged with grime

and shoe marks. She hoped her daughter would never have to work in a place like this. A job at Value Mart had been her last resort. She had filled out the application and accepted the position two days after her visit to the Tanglewood County Department of Health. *"You're eight weeks pregnant...do you know who the father is?"*

The first person Jillian had told was Alex. "Don't worry. I'll take care of you," he'd promised, holding her in his arms while she cried. Alex had kept his word. That was the type of guy he was.

Jillian glanced to her left at the sound of approaching footsteps. "Hey, Tanya," she said to the petite, rail-thin brunette with braces. "You seen Alex?"

Tanya seemed unusually nervous: hands on her tiny hips, drumming her fingertips against her studded belt. "No. Why? Is he supposed to be coming by here?"

Jillian tossed the empty can of Pringles onto a shelf close to the ground, where she sat like a garden statue. "Yeah. He'll be here later, but I'm kinda hoping he decides to rescue me sooner than we planned." She extended a hand up to Tanya. "Help me up, will you?"

Tanya obliged, struggling to heave Jillian back up to her feet.

Jillian fluffed up the back of her hair, brushed remnant crumbs from the front of her red, white, and blue sleeveless Value Mart smock.

Tanya suddenly glanced down both sides of the aisle as if she were making certain they were alone, out of earshot of gossipy coworkers and customers. She leaned in toward Jillian and whispered, "I need to tell you something. It's about Mr. LaMont."

The seriousness in Tanya's voice shot a chill down Jillian's spine. It was a premonition of sorts, as if she knew something terrible was about to happen. Jillian felt her breath quicken as she tried to dismiss the intensity of her feelings and said, jokingly, "Are you pregnant, too?"

Tanya's blue eyes grew a little wider. Her left hand went up to her ear and she toyed with one of her silver hoop earrings. "Jillian, he was *here*."

The panic began to pour through Jillian. She felt it in her chest, spreading like brush fire. Her palms started to sweat, strands of hair stuck to the back of her neck. *Stay calm*, she told herself. *This has nothing to do with you*. She feared the answer when she asked Tanya, "At the store?"

Tanya looked as if she might cry when she replied, "Yes."

Jillian's face paled. Her heart started rattling, pulsing like a pounding knock on a closed door. She placed a protective hand over her belly, certain her baby was realizing she was scared. "When?"

Realizing Jillian was concerned, Tanya said quickly, "George said he came in a few minutes ago."

"For what?"

Tanya's shoulders tightened with tension. She wiped the corners of her mouth with a shaking hand. "I'm not sure if I should tell you. I don't want you to get upset. You're pregnant and—"

"Did he buy something, Tanya?" The girl was silent. It seemed like she desperately wanted to speak, but couldn't get her words out. Jillian pushed on. "What did he buy?"

Tanya's voice cracked when she answered, "A Winchester."

Jillian felt the back of her knees weaken. The shelves around them seemed to be caving in; the aisle was shutting tight like a mouth devouring food. "A rifle? They sold Harley a *gun*?"

"I just heard about it—"

On impulse, Jillian started to move. Tanya followed quickly, trying to keep up. Jillian hurried down the aisle, toward a wider main aisle cutting across the store from front to back. "I want you to call the police."

Tanya could barely breathe. "What?"

The words of a desperate man rang in Jillian's mind, catapulted from the grounds of her memory. *"If you ever try to leave me, I'll go crazy...don't worry, I know your work schedule by heart...I'll know where to find you."*

A grave realization flooded Jillian in a cold flash. She said it aloud, terrified by her own words: "I switched schedules."

Tanya's jaw clenched with confusion. "I don't understand."

Jillian and Tanya reached the main aisle. They stood in the center, both of their eyes darting around, frightened. Jillian tried to get her thoughts out calmly. "Today is Friday. I usually work from seven until midnight. I came in at four instead. I switched schedules with Amber." Jillian looked around, her head snapping from right to left. She scanned the faces of the shoppers, searching their eyes to make certain none of them were him. She turned back to Tanya. "What time is it?"

Tanya checked the watch on her wrist. "It's almost seven o'clock."

Jillian closed her eyes for a brief second, whispered a silent prayer. She knew what Harley was capable of. He wasn't a good man, he never had been. Now he'd probably been pushed over the edge by that stupid news story Sue Ellen had talked about. Jillian feared Harley had snapped. Now she'd be his retaliation against his public humiliation.

A single tear ran down Jillian's cheek. Terror was rising inside of her. "Go, Tanya. Call the police. *Hurry.*"

Tanya turned around and ran toward the back of the store where the break room was. Jillian moved cautiously, heading toward the main entrance. Once she reached the end of the main aisle, she'd be in the front of the store, near the banks of cash registers. Close to store security.

I need to tell someone, she thought. *No. Just get out of the store. Get out of the store and run.*

Jillian hesitated as she reached a crossroads. There were aisles on each side of her. Her eyes darted quickly to her right, then to her left, searching for Harley's face in the swarm of shoppers. *Keep moving. He isn't here.*

Jillian struggled to hold back her tears. She begged God, asked him to get her out of the store alive. She made promises to him, bartered and negotiated. She thought about Chicago: the skyscrapers, the snow, the new life with Alex and Robby. She pictured herself walking out of the store and into the parking lot where Alex would be waiting for her with that adorable, dimpled smile of his.

Jillian walked past another aisle, focused on her escape. She could hear the electronic beeps of the cash registers, smell waves of the humid air outside as the automatic doors slid open and shut. Jillian didn't take the time to stop and check if he was lurking around the corners. She was fearless, spurred on by her desire to live. She'd just passed a display of pink and white hula hoops, skirted around the cardboard set-up plunked down in the middle of the main aisle where customers couldn't avoid it.

She felt Harley behind her.

His arm snaked around her neck, gripping her tight and squeezing the air out of her body. He pulled her back toward him and the fine hairs on his arm tickled her skin. She felt his belt buckle dig into the small of her back as they collided. He was dressed like he was going to work, late for class in a white Oxford and khaki slacks. The sleeves on his dress shirt were rolled up to the elbow.

"There you are," he said, as if she were a child who'd been lost somewhere in the store.

"Harley, don't," she begged.

"Have you seen the news? It's all over the place. On the Internet. My picture." His words crawled into her right ear. Her chest tightened. They started to walk, fast. They were already nearing the front of the store. Customers were concerned—they could tell something was wrong. Jillian pleaded with the faces she passed, trying to ask them for help with her eyes. They stared back at her as she was whisked by. Harley was only a few inches taller than her. He wasn't a big guy—it would be easy for someone to overtake him.

He isn't as strong as he looks. Somebody, help me.

Harley was directly behind Jillian and she was his shield. His left hand was pressed flat against the middle of her spine, guiding and forcing her. The left side of his face brushed against her right ear. She felt the front of his solid chest bang against the back of her right shoulder blade with each frenzied step they took. In a strange sense, it reminded Jillian of the time they'd had sex, a million years ago when she was his adoring student and he was the married English teacher with a sexy permanent five o'clock shadow.

"You're out of your fucking mind," she told him. "Let go of me."

"We're leaving," he insisted.

"No." It was then she felt the tip of the rifle. Harley had it in his right hand, at his side. He lifted the gun, pointed it upward and across the front of her body at a diagonal. He jammed the gun so hard beneath Jillian's chin she bit her tongue and blood began to flow from the left corner of her mouth.

Pandemonium broke out in the aisle. People began to scream, panic, run, as the reality of the situation kicked in.

Jillian and Harley reached the end of the aisle. It opened out to the front bay of the store. Jillian searched the entrance, praying.

Slivers of spit flew from his mouth when he spoke. "You ruined everything for me, you fucking bitch. My family. My career. My future."

A chubby-faced, balding security guard approached them. "Sir, we don't want any trouble here."

"I'm sorry," Jillian wheezed, feeling a thin line of blood swim down her chin.

Harley's hand moved from Jillian's spine and up to the back of her head. He grabbed a fistful of her hair and yanked as hard as he could. Harley yelled the words, "You're coming with me! Just like I said you would!"

"Okay," she said, as hot tears splashed down the sides of her face. "I'll go with you," she tried to convince him. "I'll go with you. Just don't hurt anybody, Harley. *Please.*"

A chorus of words circled around Jillian, flying at her from different directions: *"Oh my God, he has a gun" "That's them! The teacher and the student!" "Someone needs to do something. She's pregnant!"*

Jillian closed her eyes. In her mind, she was back in the examining room, at the Department of Health. She could almost smell the wretched breath of the doctor, a mixture of garlic and onions and decay. *"You're eight weeks pregnant... do you know who the father is?"* At the time, Jillian wanted to answer the question with, *"His name is Harley LaMont...he's the only man I've ever loved...except my father."*

"Why did you turn against me?" Harley demanded, ripping strands of hair out her head with a second, harder tug.

"I didn't. I swear." From the corner of her right eye, Jillian watched as the automatic doors of the entrance slid open. "No," she choked. Alex walked into the store, with a warm smile shining on his beautiful, soft face. "Oh God," Jillian whimpered at the sight of him.

Within seconds, Jillian saw the expression on Alex's face immediately shift as he registered what was happening. He locked eyes with Jillian.

"Everybody stay back!" Harley shrieked to customers and her coworkers.

At the sight of Alex, Harley loosened the grip he had on Jillian's hair. "Alex, you're not supposed to be here!" he bellowed.

"Harley, let her go," Alex insisted.

Jillian swallowed before she spoke. "Alex, where's Robby?"

Alex was struggling to maintain his composure, his calm. "He's in the car. Waiting."

"Take my car and go," she pleaded. "Turn around, Alex. *Leave*."

"No." He shook his head as fear filled his warm eyes. "I can't do that."

"Harley, listen to me," she said, trying to hide the terror from rumbling in her voice. "Don't do anything stupid, all right? This is about you and me."

Jillian looked at Alex, and she knew he was scared. She also knew he was incredibly loyal. He would never leave her to die.

"You're wrong, Jillian," Harley said. "This isn't just about you and me. This…is about *everything*."

A thousand things happened within the sliver of a second. A woman emerged from the depths of the crowd, running toward the gun, calling out Jillian's name. Robby's face somehow appeared in the swamp of scared faces and he started crying.

The security guard took a brave step forward, moving in on Harley.

In her belly, Jillian felt her baby kick the outer ridges of her soul. As Jillian started to scream, Harley aimed the gun, pulled the trigger, and fired.

Twice.

ALEX

It took a few seconds for Alex to register what had happened, for the brutal reality to sink in.

Harley was dead, killed by his own bullet. The second shot.

Jillian had been hit by his first bullet. But she was still alive.

Just barely.

A surge of adrenaline soared through his body, moving him on impulse, guiding him by sheer instinct. Alex forced his way through the crowd gathering around her. He shoved them out of his path, elbowing their sides. "Get back!" he shrieked. "Get the fuck away from her!"

He dropped to his knees, falling to the ground beside his best friend. He reached for her and saw the blood. It was pumping out of a hole in her shoulder. "Somebody help me!" Alex begged.

Jillian made a soft gurgling sound. "Alex," she breathed. "Don't let me die in this place." Tears slid from the corners of her eyes and dripped to the ground smudged with shoeprints, mixing with the growing puddle of blood beneath her body.

Giselle appeared next to them, down on one knee, leaning over Jillian's body. It was then Alex remembered seeing the school nurse moments before, what she'd done in the split second before the first bullet was fired. She'd broken through the crowd and dived in Jillian's direction. But Giselle couldn't move fast enough. No one could.

The security guard was on his cell phone, shouting instructions. "Get the ambulance here now!" he yelled to the 911 operator.

Sue Ellen rushed forward with pillows, ripping their plastic packaging off with her hands. She shoved them at Alex, shaking. He took them from her, gently guiding them beneath Jillian's head. He turned to the security guard, panicked. "Where's the ambulance?"

"They're here," he insisted. "They're in the parking lot."

"She's bleeding all over the fucking place!" Alex shouted.

Giselle reached up and yanked a floral printed blouse from a hanger. She balled the shirt up in her hands and pressed it hard against Jillian's wound. "Get these people out of here," she instructed. She looked up at Sue Ellen. "These people don't need to see this. Do something."

Sue Ellen snapped into form. "Everybody get back!" The crowd of onlookers reluctantly obeyed, shifting in one large wave, retreating toward the cash registers. "Have some respect, people!"

"Alex?" the familiar voice said in the near distance.

Alex looked up and saw Robby standing next to Harley's lifeless body. Tears were spilling down his cheeks. Alex's eyes shifted to Jillian, and he watched as Robby's heart broke right in front of him.

"No," he pleaded through his sobs. "No."

"Robby, I need you to be strong right now. You hear me?"

Robby nodded, wiped his cheeks with the back of his

hand. He rushed to Alex's side, slipping his hand into Jillian's. "I love you," he whispered to her. And Alex knew it was the truth.

He knew Jillian believed Robby, too. She struggled to lift her head up to reach the side of his face, his ear. "I'm not getting out of here," she said to him. Her voice was weak, breathy. Alex didn't like the sound of it. She was losing the fight for her life—and he knew it. "Take care of Alex for me."

Robby kissed her cheek softly. "Always," he promised.

She lowered her head and offered Giselle a soft smile. "Thank you," she said.

"Anything for you, angel," Giselle replied, losing the struggle to hold her tears back.

Alex saw the flash of lights outside of the store. A swirling storm of pulsating white and blue and the urgent wail of the anxious sirens brought comfort to him.

The store was invaded within seconds. Men and women in uniforms with silver badges and gun holsters swarmed the place, ushering the crowd away from Harley and Jillian—forcing everyone far away from the scene of the crime.

The paramedics followed in next, rushing to get to Jillian, trying to save her.

Alex felt strong arms on his body, pulling him away from Jillian. He shouted in protest, struggling violently. "Let go of me," he begged with everything he had left.

Jillian sensed his absence. She made a soft moaning sound, tilted her head back, pressing it deeper into the soft white pillow. She started to convulse. Blood bubbled out of her mouth, trickling down the sides of her face and chin.

"We're losing her here!" Giselle screamed to anyone who would listen.

Jillian was surrounded by strangers intent on saving her

life. Alex knew his best friend needed these people more than anyone else in the world.

He swallowed his rage and reached for Robby, pulling him into his arms, sobbing into the sleeve of Robby's gray sweatshirt.

Seconds later, Alex felt Giselle's hand on his back. He turned and met her eyes. "Go with her," she urged. He stared at her blankly, confused. "The ambulance," she continued, cutting through his cloud of grief. "Robby and I will meet you there...at the hospital."

Alex nodded, absorbing the meaning of the woman's words, drinking the small amount of hope he heard in them. *The hospital? An ambulance? Maybe they're going to save her. Maybe Jillian will be okay.*

But as Alex scrambled into the back of the ambulance and clutched Jillian's hand, he saw how pale she looked—like she was already a ghost—and he knew.

It's only a matter of time.

"My baby," she said, her words muffled by an oxygen mask.

Alex turned and looked for an answer from the uniformed woman in the ambulance with them. "The baby's vitals are fine," she reassured Alex.

Alex touched Jillian's cheek softly with the back of his hand. "Did you hear that, Jilli?"

"My baby," she repeated.

Alex held his best friend's hand, unsure if he'd ever be able to let go. "She's fine," he told her. "Your baby is okay."

Jillian squeezed Alex's hand in response. He was surprised by her strength.

❖

They were trying to make him leave the room, but Alex refused. He'd run alongside the gurney, from the ambulance, down the hospital corridor, and through doors that buzzed before swinging open.

He wouldn't let go of Jillian's hand. No one in the world could make him.

"I won't leave her!" Alex told the nurse.

"Sir, you need to wait outside."

"No." He shook his head, tasting his own tears. "No. I won't go."

Something happened in the room, causing the attention to shift from Alex and back to Jillian. A machine she'd been connected to was flashing and beeping—emitting a serious warning of some kind.

A doctor rushed into the room, and for a moment Alex wondered if it was his mother he was seeing. The resemblance between her and the doctor was startling.

Jillian stirred, and her voice was panicked. "What's happening to me?" she asked. "Alex?"

He looked at the doctor, standing on the opposite side of Jillian's bed. Alex locked eyes with her and asked, "Is it the baby?"

The doctor nodded in silence before she leaned over Jillian and said in a gentle tone, "Jillian? I'm Dr. Petrosian."

"My baby," Jillian responded. "Please, lady…help my baby."

"We need to operate, Jillian. We need your permission to perform a surgery to save your baby."

Jillian nodded. "Yes…do whatever you have to." Jillian turned her head slowly, her eyes searching for Alex. "Tell her, Alex," she said.

A petite nurse appeared next to Dr. Petrosian, holding a

clipboard and a pen. "Jillian," the doctor continued, "I need you to answer a question for me."

Jillian didn't take her eyes off Alex. Something inside him knew not to break their stare, not to look away. They spoke volumes in only the slivers of seconds passing.

"Jillian, we need to know who the father of the child is."

Alex's eyes swelled with tears, mirroring the intense wave of emotion floating in Jillian's eyes. Without a word, they knew it was good-bye.

"Jillian," the doctor repeated, with more urgency in her voice. "Who is the father of your baby?"

Like best friends often do, Jillian and Alex spoke at the same time, in perfect unison.

"He is," Jillian said without taking her eyes off him.

"I am," Alex declared. His words were spoken with more pride than he'd ever felt in his life.

"Very well," Dr. Petrosian concluded. "Sir, we have some paperwork we need for you to sign."

Alex's fingertips trembled as he reached for Jillian's cheek, brushing her tears away, allowing her sorrow to be absorbed into his own skin.

"Sir," the doctor prompted.

Alex nodded, still locking eyes with Jillian. *"Haskanum em,"* he said, more to his best friend than to the doctor.

He could feel the doctor's smile, lighting up the room and covering his skin with warmth and kindness. "I see," she said. She continued in Armenian, filling the space around them with the native tongue of Alex's mother, his ancestors. His history. The doctor assumed he spoke the language, so he continued to smile and nod.

When they separated Alex from Jillian and their hands drifted apart, Alex sensed his mother's presence. He felt her standing next to him, watching as Jillian was rolled away and taken to an operating room.

He closed his eyes, imagining her there with him. Her soft hands. Her gentle waves of laughter. Her sad, beautiful gaze. The always-present loneliness in her warm voice.

"Mom," Alex said to the empty hospital room. "Take care of her for me."

Alex felt his heart break an hour later when he remembered he'd slipped Jillian's wishes into his front pocket earlier in the day in her bedroom. He fished out the box with the Chinese writing on it, lifted the lid, and reached inside for a piece of paper. He unfolded it and stared down at Jillian's words, scrawled against white. He blinked back hot tears as he discovered what mattered most to his best friend.

I don't want my baby to grow up in Georgia. I never want her to feel unloved.

Dr. Petrosian came to them in the waiting room then, found them sitting in plastic chairs, thumbing mindlessly through year-old issues of magazines, hoping.

Alex stood and shoved the wish box back into his pocket. He breathed in deep. He clutched Robby's hand tightly in his. He waited. He tasted hope. But it melted down the back of his throat and burned with bitterness.

When Delilah Dambro collapsed into the comforting arms of Alex's father and sobbed hysterically at the news that her daughter had just died, Alex felt his world was permanently destroyed. Even Robby couldn't comfort him, no matter how hard he tried. There was nothing anyone could say or do to repair the damage done to Alex's soul.

Jillian was gone.

But the kind doctor urged Alex to come with her. So he followed the hope in her voice to the maternity ward, to the nursery, to a maze of incubators and babies and nurses. And one of them—an older woman who smelled like roses—she placed a newborn baby into Alex's open arms, saying, "Here's your daddy."

He took the child and a wave of love flooded his heart, temporarily holding his drowning grief at bay. He held the baby close to him, amazed by how tiny she was, how much she needed him.

Alex wasn't sure of what to do, what to say. He'd never held a baby before. Maybe the nurse could tell how overwhelmed he was because she offered him some advice: "Just use your instincts. You'll know what to do."

He knew at once he shared an unbreakable connection with the delicate little girl in his arms. He could tell just by looking down at her.

Just as he had, she'd inherited her mother's beautiful eyes.

MARTHA

There was no question: Martha knew she had to be there. Once she received the texted words from John—what Harley had done and that Jillian was fighting for her life and the life of her baby—she dismissed her dance class early, rented a car and drove six hours straight from Amelia Island, Florida, to Harmonville, Georgia.

But halfway there, Martha had to pull over. She hurried out of the car and rushed to the side of the road. Where the shoulder and asphalt ended was a sloped embankment filled with the most gorgeous wildflowers Martha had ever seen. The colors were so vibrant, she couldn't help but wonder if someone had painted them in purple, white, and pink. They reached up to her knees. She stood, clutching her stomach and staring at the tops of the flowers. She felt the hot sun beating down on the back of her head, as if God were reprimanding her and contemplating her punishment. A wave of nausea rocked her body and she knew she was going to be sick.

John hadn't sent any details in his text, but Martha couldn't help but feel terribly guilty. She thought back to that night—New Year's Eve—when she'd found a distraught and shivering Jillian standing on her front lawn, her eyes transfixed on Harley's ominous silhouette in the upstairs window.

I could have stopped it then. I could have saved her. None of this would have happened if I had stayed. If I had destroyed Harley myself.

The smell the highway flowers were emitting was sweet and powerful. They soothed Martha's soul, calming her, instilling in her a sense of deep purpose.

She straightened her body, stared out to the endless horizon. She knew there was no one else in Harmonville who could handle the aftermath of what Harley had done. She was the only person who had the strength it would require to piece everyone back together, even if only temporarily. No one else would have the capabilities of coordinating the funerals, especially if there had to be one for a teenaged girl.

Martha returned to the car, wiped her eyes, and whispered a prayer. She knew she was a strong woman, but she begged for God's help and for Jillian's life to be saved.

She pulled back onto the highway and glanced in her rearview mirror. Despite how much she loved and cared for the people she had left behind five months ago in Harmonville, there was a part of Martha that couldn't wait to return to her new life in Amelia Island.

As she drove, Martha reflected back on the eleven years she had known Harley. How could a man she had once loved so much turn into such a monster? What had sent him over the edge, to the point he wanted to kill?

Martha was a single mom eleven years ago, struggling to get by when she'd met an unshaven Harley in the grocery store. He was standing in the produce section with a cantaloupe in his hand, staring at it and inspecting it like it was the head of an alien. Martha had smiled to herself, amused by how cute and helpless Harley appeared. She approached him and explained one way to tell if a cantaloupe was ripe: smell it. He did as she instructed and he nodded and placed the fruit in his cart. They talked for a while. She explained she had a seven-year-old and was a receptionist. He talked about being a graduate student at a nearby university and being lonely in Pittsburgh. They exchanged numbers, and three nights later, they had their first date. Five months later, they were married in a small, no-frills wedding. From that moment on, Martha's life had never been the same.

In the beginning, Harley was romantic and kind, doting on her and constantly showering her with affection. But once he began teaching, Martha's world shifted. Gone were the flowers and poetry, replaced by constant criticism and a frustrated strain in every word he spoke. Martha soon felt she couldn't do anything right, no matter how hard she tried. Harley would never be happy, not with anything or anyone. Nothing could measure up to the impossible expectations he set for her.

Martha shook the memory away, turned up the car radio, and concentrated on the long drive. When she arrived in Harmonville, she was exhausted and heavy with concern. She pulled into the hospital lot, parked the car, and sat for a moment, motionless. Only able to breathe.

Martha worried she wouldn't be able to face John. She'd left him without a good-bye. And her own son, abandoned by his own mother to fend for himself. To deal with Harley's moods, his new relationship with Alex.

How could I have left my own child behind? And John? The only man who's ever really loved me. My God...what have I done?

❖

Martha reentered their lives only seconds after death had arrived, shaking their worlds, rattling and breaking their hearts. She rushed past John and reached for Alex and Robby.

She pulled the boys to her and refused to let go until their sobs subsided. All the while, she whispered words of comfort to Delilah, whom John was doing his best to hold up.

Finally, Delilah crumbled in a chair in the waiting room, demanding, "Why would he do this to her? He was her teacher."

Martha sat next to the woman, squeezed her hands, brushed the tears from her cheeks. She sent John to get coffee from a vending machine. The boys sat across from her, enveloped in each other's arms.

"She was a good girl," Delilah sobbed. "She never hurt nobody." Delilah's eyes moved to Alex, as if he were the only person in the waiting room who understood what she was saying. "Alex," she stammered, "what am I going to do now? She was all I had."

"No," he said, shaking his head. "You have a granddaughter now."

A beam of hope started to shine in Delilah's bloodshot eyes.

Martha turned and asked, "Is the baby okay?"

"She's fine," he said. "My daughter is fine."

Martha gave him a look of confusion. "*Your* daughter?"

Alex nodded, tightened his grip on Robby, who still cried. "Yes," he reiterated. "*My* daughter."

It wasn't until early morning that Alex explained to her what had happened in the hospital room. They were standing on the front porch. Across the street stood the house Martha had once shared with Harley. Now the house looked terrifying, haunted, a place of evil. Her wicked, sad life with Harley felt like it was a hundred years ago.

"There's no other choice," Alex said to her, leaning against the white balustrade. The air smelled sweet and sticky. Honeysuckle had recently bloomed. The scent made Martha feel dizzy. "People assumed the kid was mine anyways. A lot of people at school thought we were in love."

"But the baby isn't yours, Alex…not biologically. As much as I hate to say it, Harley was the father," Martha reminded him.

Alex's eyes flashed. "And where is he now?"

Martha sighed, feeling her shoulders relax a little as she sat in the porch swing and started to rock gently. "Good point," she agreed.

"No one wants the baby except for me," he continued.

Martha shot him a look. "That isn't true."

"So you want to take her back to Florida or wherever it is you've been hiding all these months? You think my dad wants to get up in the middle of the night to change a diaper? Or do you want her to end up at some orphanage or in a foster home?"

Martha lowered her eyes, feeling ashamed. "I understand."

"No, the baby isn't *mine*," he explained. "But she is now. I signed papers at the hospital. Jillian told the doctor I was the father."

"This is what she wanted?"

He nodded in the moonlight. "Yes."

"Then I won't interfere. It certainly isn't my place." Martha stood up, prepared to go into the house. She'd been avoiding John since she arrived. Except for giving him a hug at the hospital and assuring him, "We'll get through this somehow," she hadn't said a word to him.

"I know why you're here now," Alex said, stopping her

a second before she was at the front door, her hand on the screen. "Why in the hell did you leave in the first place?"

Martha had no answer for him. She simply replied, "I'm here now, Alex." She went inside to find John waiting for her. He was sitting in a recliner in the living room, his eyes heavy and tired.

Martha had few words of explanation for John when he posed the question to her: "Where you been, Martha?"

She didn't respond. Instead, she went to him, bent down, and slid her arms around him. He stood up from his favorite chair and held her. Only then did Martha allow herself to cry.

❖

Martha took control of everything. She unofficially elected herself to be the person in charge.

And there was so much to do.

First, she made the funeral arrangements, agreeing with Alex's request that Jillian's body be cremated. "I want to take her ashes with us when we leave," he told her.

"Leave?" she repeated back. "Where are you and Robby going?"

Martha resisted at first when she was informed Alex and Robby were intent on moving to Chicago, to start a new life there. She questioned them, voicing concerns that they were too young, they had never been on their own before, Chicago was so far away and the winters there were brutal.

Once Robby and Alex assured her this was what they wanted more than anything in the world, and they explained to her how they had planned this move originally with Jillian and the baby in mind, Martha not only gave in, she took on their cause.

Martha organized their entire move. She reserved a moving truck, helped them pack their things, made them care packages—one for the ride there, the other to open when they got there. She searched the Web with them, narrowing down the best choices for an apartment. She even called their perspective landlords, grilled them for info, and negotiated their rent, lowering the monthly payment by nearly a hundred dollars.

The boys were illuminated, euphoric with their escape plan. Their eyes were constantly filled with excitement. They talked endlessly about what their life would be like. They strategized and discussed their visions in great detail. Martha watched from the outside, realizing that Robby had never looked so happy.

❖

Harley's funeral came and went with no reaction from anyone. Martha took care of the details: the plot, the headstone, the flowers. She let the high school principal know. He informed her, "We're sorry for your loss, ma'am, but I don't expect anyone from our school will be attending the service." That was same reaction Martha received from Harley's distant relatives—his cousins in Maine, a half sister in Hawaii, a former college roommate in Pittsburgh. No one wanted to come, but they all wished her well. It seemed to Martha the world was a happier place without Harley LaMont. His lust for teenaged girls was sending him to his grave as a man best forgotten.

Martha decided not to go to the cemetery and stand graveside as Harley was lowered into the ground. It was an agonizing decision for her, but she hoped Harley would somehow realize how alone he had made her feel. She wanted him to know about the damage he had done—that the lives he'd tried to ruin would go on without him.

❖

Nearly two hundred people attended Jillian's service, held at a local church. Inside, white flowers draped the sanctuary. A lifetime's worth of photos of Jillian were on display.

People Martha had never met before—mostly high school students—sobbed through Alex's heartfelt eulogy. He spoke of the meaning of friendship, articulated how much Jillian meant to him, to his life, and how much she would impact his future.

Mrs. Gregory was there, and so was Giselle. Tommy Freeman and his older sister Sue Ellen sat together in a pew. Tommy tried his best to comfort Sue Ellen, but it was no use. The siblings were dressed in black, and they held each other's hands as they walked out of church, grief pressing down on their hearts and backs.

Martha helped Delilah Dambro to her feet while the devastated mother cried out for her dead daughter, teetering in her black heels. Martha helped Delilah into a limousine, promising Delilah she'd check in on her from time to time, to make sure she was okay. Delilah nodded through her tears and thanked Martha profusely, almost desperately.

On the front steps of the church, Martha watched as Alex and Robby embraced. As they pulled away from each other, she saw the beautiful tenderness in their eyes, their shared love reflecting in their gazes. She knew the two of them would be okay.

As long as they had each other.

❖

Emily Siran Bainbridge was brought home from the hospital twelve days after she was born.

Martha took it upon herself to load the boys up with everything they'd need to properly care for Emily: a car seat, a crib, a stroller, clothes, bottles, diapers, and plenty of food. She reminded them constantly about how important it would be for them to find a pediatrician as soon as they got to Chicago. She rambled on to them about vaccinations, the importance of keeping records and paperwork, sleep deprivation, and how to cope with teething, diaper rash, potty training, and anything and everything else she could possibly think of.

"You know I'll be visiting you every other month," she told them in the driveway the morning they were packed and ready to leave.

John had agreed to drive the moving truck to Chicago and help the boys unpack. Alex and Robby would follow in John's car, with baby Emily in tow.

Martha hugged them both, afraid to let go.

"I love you both," she said into their necks, hoping her words would somehow dissolve into their skin and remain there forever.

While John was gone in Chicago, Martha kept busy. She put Harley's house on the market, set up a trust fund for Emily, called the boys every hour on the hour, and checked on Delilah daily.

When John returned, she met him on the front porch. She was sitting on the porch swing, drinking a cup of coffee. He was exhausted, and she knew it. But they were finally alone. She gestured for him to sit beside her, and he did.

"There's no one here but us now," she said. "It's strange."

John was silent for a moment before he spoke. "You have a lot of explaining to do, Martha," he said to her. "You broke my heart when you left without a word. Not even a good-bye."

Martha's eyes closed. The hurt in John's voice was almost unbearable. "I don't think I can ever explain to you why I left," she answered. "I only know…it's what I had to do."

He turned and looked at her. She felt his eyes on her, questioning and scared. "And now?"

She took a sip of coffee and said, "I put Harley's house on the market while you were gone."

His voice cracked with a smile. "Does this mean you're moving in with me?"

"Not quite," she replied. Martha took a deep breath, then: "I'm going back to Amelia Island, John. I have an incredible life there. I've opened a dance studio. It's something I've always wanted to do."

He swallowed. "So, is this good-bye?"

She reached for his hand, covered it with hers. "I hope not," she replied.

"What *are* you hoping for?" he asked.

She smiled. Her bottom lip trembled. "That you'll come with me."

He turned and their eyes met. "Is that what you really want?"

Martha nodded. "More than anything."

"Leave Harmonville?" he wondered aloud. "It sounds like a great idea to me."

Martha kissed his mouth softly. "We need to leave, John. This place is haunted. Too many ghosts."

He put an arm around her, pulled her closer to his body,

and held her. "Give me two days to tie up some loose ends," he said.

"I'll give you as much time as you need," she told him. "You're definitely worth the wait, John Bainbridge."

September/September

ALEX

Alex purposely asked Robby to meet him on the steps of the Art Institute on Michigan Avenue. He was very specific in the text message he'd sent him over an hour ago.

While he waited for Robby to arrive with their daughter, Alex sat on the cement steps outside of the majestic museum, welcoming the warmth of the sun on his skin. He watched the throng of tourists, college students, the corporate clones in business suits. They moved together in a sea of camera flashes, drinking in the beauty and marvel of the place, awed. It was impossible to walk by the museum and not be touched by the grandness of it.

Alex thought of his mother then. He wondered what the moment felt like for her when she had laid eyes on John Bainbridge for the first time, over twenty years ago. Alex was curious where his mother was standing or sitting when it happened. He hoped it was in the exact spot where he sat, waiting for Robby LaMont to appear—the love of *his* life.

For a moment, Alex imagined his mother was sitting on one of the concrete steps below his. She was smiling, drinking in the sights and sounds of her favorite city, high from the hope shining in her eyes. She waved at him, gestured at him to come to her, to sit beside her. He obeyed and moved through the crowd to join the ghostly vision of his mother.

What thoughts were running through your mind, Mom? Was it love at first sight for you? How much English did you speak back then? What were the first words you spoke to your future husband, the man who would become my father?

"Yes kez sirumem," his mother replied, in his mind.

Alex wasn't sure if she was answering his question, or simply reminding him of what she felt in her heart for him. So he responded with, "I love you, too."

Sensing Robby had arrived, Alex looked up and saw him standing motionless in the center of the crowd. He was a beautiful rock, sturdy and solid, as a constant flow of activity whirled around him in hyper-speed. Robby was holding on for dear life to the handles of Emily's stroller, with elbows locked and his jaw tight.

Alex stood up. He moved toward them, taking each step slowly, as if every movement he made had a significant purpose.

Once he reached them, Alex leaned in to Robby and kissed his cheek. "Hello, beautiful," he greeted him.

"How was the first day of class?" Robby asked, his tone anxious. His hair was much shorter than it had been in Harmonville. They both looked a little older, as responsibility helped them transition from boys to men.

"I think I'm in love," Alex replied.

Robby raised an eyebrow. "Do I have competition?" he said, with a smile.

"I don't know. Columbia College is pretty awesome."

"And your classes?"

"I love 'em." Alex beamed. "Not as much as I love you, though. And this little angel you have with you."

"She threw up on the train," Robby offered. "It was like *The Exorcist.*"

"Classy." Alex laughed. "And one of my all-time favorite horror films."

"I think I fed her too much again," Robby worried.

"We're parents in training," Alex reminded him. "Let's go out tonight and celebrate."

"How? We have no sitter."

"Already taken care of."

Robby grinned. "Your cousins?"

"My aunts," Alex said. "They're insisting Emily be fluent in Armenian by her first birthday."

"Where should we go?"

"Wherever you want," Alex said. "We're not just celebrating my first day of school."

"No?"

"We've lived here for four months now," Alex said.

"So it's an anniversary...of sorts," Robby concluded.

"I think every day we should celebrate something," Alex suggested.

"Yeah," Robby agreed. "I like that."

"C'mon," Alex urged. They started to walk, heading toward Millennium Park. "Let's spend the afternoon with our daughter. Then the three of us can watch the sunset."

They made their way down Michigan Avenue. Occasionally, Alex stole glances at Robby. Each time he looked at the beautiful man walking beside him, Alex felt breathless—the same way he'd felt the first time they met in his driveway over a year ago. The same shudder he'd experienced when Robby and he had first kissed was still rippling inside his soul—just at the sight of him.

Robby LaMont made Alex Bainbridge feel the same intoxicating high he felt whenever he turned to the sky—a wild exhilaration that anything was possible. Much like Alex used to feel whenever he was swimming to his island, kicking and propelling himself through the water, hoping when he emerged and broke the surface of the lake, he'd find love waiting for him.

But now Alex was in Chicago.

He'd finally come home.

Now, he was coming up for air.

About the Author

David-Matthew Barnes is the author of the young adult novels *Mesmerized* and *Swimming to Chicago*, and the literary suspense novel *Accidents Never Happen*, all published by Bold Strokes Books. He wrote and directed the coming-of-age film *Frozen Stars*, which received worldwide distribution. He is the author of over forty stage plays that have been performed in three languages in eight countries. His literary work has appeared in over one hundred publications including *The Best Stage Scenes*, *The Best Men's Stage Monologues*, *The Best Women's Stage Monologues*, *The Comstock Review*, *Review Americana*, and *The Southeast Review*. David-Matthew is the national recipient of the 2011 Hart Crane Memorial Poetry Award. In addition, he's received the Carrie McCray Literary Award and the Slam Boston Award for Best Play, and has earned double awards for poetry and playwriting in the World AIDS Day Writing Contest. David-Matthew earned a Master of Fine Arts in creative writing at Queens University of Charlotte in North Carolina. He lives in Griffin, Georgia, where he is a faculty member at Southern Crescent Technical College.

Soliloquy Titles From Bold Strokes Books

Swimming to Chicago by David-Matthew Barnes. As the lives of the adults around them unravel, high school students Alex and Robby form an unbreakable bond, vowing to do anything to stay together—even if it means leaving everything behind. (978-1-60282-572-7)

Speaking Out edited by Steve Berman. Inspiring stories written for and about LGBT and Q teens of overcoming adversity (against intolerance and homophobia) and experiencing life after "coming out." (978-1-60282-566-6)

365 Days by K.E. Payne. Life sucks when you're seventeen years old and confused about your sexuality, and the girl of your dreams doesn't even know you exist. Then in walks sexy new emo girl, Hannah Harrison. Clemmie Atkins has exactly 365 days to discover herself, and she's going to have a blast doing it! (978-1-60282-540-6)

Cursebusters! by Julie Smith. Budding-psychic Reeno is the most accomplished teenage burglar in California, but one tiny screw-up and poof!—she's sentenced to Bad Girl School. And that isn't even her worst problem. Her sister Haley's dying of an illness no one can diagnose, and now she can't even help. (978-1-60282-559-8)

Who I Am by M.L. Rice. Devin Kelly's senior year is a disaster. She's in a new school in a new town, and the school bully is making her life miserable—but then she meets his sister Melanie and realizes her feelings for her are more than platonic. (978-1-60282-231-3)

Sleeping Angel by Greg Herren. Eric Matthews survives a terrible car accident only to find out everyone in town thinks he's a murderer—and he has to clear his name even though he has no memories of what happened. (978-1-60282-214-6)

Mesmerized by David-Matthew Barnes. Through her close friendship with Brodie and Lance, Serena Albright learns about the many forms of love and finds comfort for the grief and guilt she feels over the brutal death of her older brother, the victim of a hate crime. (978-1-60282-191-0)

The Perfect Family by Kathryn Shay. A mother and her gay son stand hand in hand as the storms of change engulf their perfect family and the life they knew. (978-1-60282-181-1)

Father Knows Best by Lynda Sandoval. High school juniors and best friends Lila Moreno, Meryl Morganstern, and Caressa Thibodoux plan to make the most of the summer before senior year. What they discover that amazing summer about girl power, growing up, and trusting friends and family more than prepares them to tackle that all-important senior year! (978-1-60282-147-7)